W9-BMP-472

DATE DUE

JUL 3 1 2015			
AUG 1 3 2015			
AUG 2 8 2015			
SEP 2 9 2015			
JAN 6 2016			
MAY 3 2016			
AUG 2 2017			
JAN 2 2018			

LP   Holmes, L.P.   2015
WES   The Crimson Hills
F
HOL

THE
CRIMSON
HILLS

Center Point
Large Print

**This Large Print Book carries the
Seal of Approval of N.A.V.H.**

THE CRIMSON HILLS

L. P. Holmes

CENTER POINT LARGE PRINT
THORNDIKE, MAINE

A Circle Ⓥ Western published by
Center Point Large Print in the year 2015
in co-operation with Golden West Literary Agency.

An earlier version of *The Crimson Hills*
first appeared under the title "The Owlhoot Angel"
in *Action Stories* (Fall, '47). Copyright © 1947
by Fiction House, Inc. Copyright © renewed 1975
by L.P. Holmes. Copyright © 2015 by Golden West
Literary Agency for restored material.

First Edition July, 2015

Printed in the United States of America
on permanent paper.
Set in 16-point Times New Roman type.

ISBN: 978-1-62899-630-2 (hardcover)
ISBN: 978-1-62899-635-7 (paperback)

Library of Congress Cataloging-in-Publication Data

Holmes, L. P. (Llewellyn Perry), 1895–1988.
 The crimson hills : a western story / L. P. Holmes.
 pages cm
 Summary: "When Dave Wall refuses to do Luke Lilavelt's dirty work
any longer, Lilavelt makes good on his threat to reveal a secret from
Dave's brother-in-law's past that could send him to prison or worse.
Now Dave has to find a way stop Lilavelt's plans"
  —Provided by publisher.
 ISBN 978-1-62899-630-2 (hardcover : alk. paper)
 ISBN 978-1-62899-635-7 (pbk. : alk. paper)
 1. Large type books. I. Title.
 PS3515.O4448C75 2015
 813′.52—dc23

2015012509

THE CRIMSON HILLS

Chapter One

The yellow glow of the hanging lamp threw hard highlights across Luke Lilavelt's bony head and shoulders, emphasizing the beaked predatoriness of his nose and chin while leaving his narrow gash of a mouth and his small, cold eyes in shadow. Restless under the solid impact of Dave Wall's settled hatred, Lilavelt stirred and jabbed a finger at the crudely drawn map spread on the table before him, while his words seeped out, thin and nasal, between lips repressed to a miserly economy of movement.

"Sure you got all this clear? I want that stretch between the Monuments and Stinking Water opened up once and for all. I'm tired of having to drive twenty miles out of my way every time I move cattle in or out of my Crimson Hills holdings. I can't seem to get any action out of Burke, so I'm sending you in to take over. Here's my written authority for that move. I want action, Wall . . . and I want it fast."

Lilavelt tossed a folded paper across the desk and Dave Wall pocketed it without even glancing at the contents, while he spoke with a slow, sarcastic emphasis.

"Maybe you're not paying Tom Burke enough money, Lilavelt. Or maybe he's fed up on doing your dirty work. Chances are, you're not fooling Burke any more than you're fooling me. You talk of opening up the barrier range between the Monuments and Stinking Water, but that's not what you're really after. What you've got your sights set on is Bart Sutton and his whole Square S layout. Someday, Lilavelt, you're going to start slipping on your own slickness and before you quit sliding, you'll end up neck deep in hell."

Lilavelt got to his feet, tall, lank, stoop-shouldered. "Any time you want to quit me, you can, Wall." Then he added, acid in his voice: "I understand there's been a new addition to the Connell family. This time a little girl. That makes twin boys and a girl. A nice family, Wall . . . yeah, a right nice little family. Be a pity to break it up, wouldn't it?"

Dave Wall was sprawled deep in his chair, all the long, rugged length of him slouched and relaxed. Only in his sun-blackened face was there a suggestion of tension and it was a settled thing that pinched the corners of his eyes slightly and compressed his wide lips with a vague bitterness. Now he said, his voice perfectly even: "Keep your mealy mouth off that family. Someday, for the sake of Judith and Jerry and the kids, I'll probably kill you."

Luke Lilavelt shrugged. "You've said that before. I'm not worrying about it. Not while I got the story of Jerry Connell's past locked up in Judge Masterson's safe in his courthouse chambers. In case of my sudden and violent demise, Judge Masterson has instructions to open that sealed envelope and act on the contents." Lilavelt's words ended on a note of glib and taunting mockery.

Dave Wall got to his feet. "Luke, you're a damned dirty, greedy, crooked rat."

It was said of Luke Lilavelt that his hide was as thick as his conscience was thin. Yet no man could have taken the whipping scorn and contempt in Dave Wall's words without some reaction. So now Lilavelt slapped an open hand sharply on the desk and his nasal drone lifted to a tight, high note.

"Cut it fine, Wall . . . cut it fine. There's nothing to stop me from sending word to Judge Masterson to open that envelope right now."

Dave Wall laughed harshly. "Oh, yes, there is. Because if you did that, it would end all reason for me letting you go on living. As things stand right now, you've got me by the short hair. But by the same token I've got you by the throat. So, if I want to call you a rat, you'll just have to take it and like it."

Which was true enough, as Lilavelt well knew. So, while with his little, sunken eyes he hated Dave Wall wickedly, Lilavelt changed the subject abruptly.

"I've sent word out to Spayd at Gravelly to

start a gather of five hundred two-year-olds. In three weeks that gather will be moving in to the Crimson Hills range. I'll expect you to have the trail open by that time."

Lilavelt turned to a rack and lifted down his battered old sweat-greased hat and the thread-bare old coat that he'd worn as far back as Dave Wall could remember him. Studying the man with shadowed eyes, Wall wondered how one human carcass could hold all the miserly greed, the venom, the lies, the sly and slimy trickery, the utter and callous ruthlessness that was bound up in Luke Lilavelt.

This man, so far as Dave Wall knew, had no living kin of any kind. To spend a dollar made Luke Lilavelt actually writhe. Yet the man was enormously wealthy. White-faced cattle, carrying Luke Lilavelt's Window Sash brand, fed on the grass of four counties. Their numbers ran into the many thousands and the combined range he controlled, if all blocked together, would have measured forty or fifty square miles. He had the power that such possessions always gave, and, well aware of this, he used that power shrewdly and without pity. Politicians listened when Luke Lilavelt spoke and lesser men of many kinds jumped at his word. Nobody liked Luke Lilavelt, but many feared him.

He had started from scratch with a shoe-string outfit. There were old-timers who claimed that

Luke Lilavelt had registered the Window Sash as his iron because it was so easy to run a Window Sash out of Hutch Horne's Double H and Bert Pryor's Cross in a Box. Be that as it might, the fact remained that Hutch Horne and Bert Pryor were long since dead, their once big and flourishing outfits just memories. And the range they once controlled were now integral parts of Luke Lilavelt's cattle kingdom.

Other big outfits had got in the way of the tide of power and control that was Luke Lilavelt and his Window Sash and had been rolled under. Little outfits were sucked in and swallowed. Their choice was simple and tragic. Sell out to Window Sash at Lilavelt's own price or be smothered and rubbed out by the power of a range piracy they did not have the strength to combat. There seemed to be no way of stopping Luke Lilavelt and his rapacious machine.

For a lot longer than he cared to think about, Dave Wall had been part of that machine, despising Luke Lilavelt and all that the man represented, despising himself equally for the part he had to play, yet knowing that his helplessness in the matter was that of an autumn leaf in the grip of stormy winds. Now Wall built a cigarette and spoke slowly.

"Sometimes, just for the hell of it, I've tried to figure you out, Luke. You haven't a friend in the world. Oh, I know there are plenty who give you

11

lip service, but in their hearts every one of them hates your guts. Like me. I work for you, I do your dirty work, but I despise you clear past hell. You've got more money now than any one man could spend legitimately in five lifetimes. Yet no dollar gets out of your hands that isn't squeezed out of shape. When you die, there'll be a celebration and men will go out of their way to spit on your grave. So far as I know . . . and I've watched pretty carefully . . . I've never seen you show or speak a kind or generous word. Just what the devil do you get out of life, anyhow?"

Lilavelt opened his office door and waited for Wall to go out for, if possible, Luke Lilavelt never let any man stand behind him where he couldn't be watched. A sardonic light burned in his crafty eyes.

"I'm not paying you to read my make-up, Wall. But as long as you asked, maybe I get quite a lift out of seeing wise *hombres* like you jump when I snap the whip. You've got your orders. Hit the trail for the Crimson Hills range and do the job I've sent you on."

This was one of the things Luke Lilavelt liked best of all—to lay the lash of his authority across the backs of other men. Dave Wall's big shoulders swung restlessly under the impact, and the ever-present but useless revolt made his words brittle.

"In good time, Luke . . . in good time."

Lilavelt locked his office door and turned off

downstreet, throwing a reedy reminder over his shoulder. "You've got a job to do. Get at it!"

Dave Wall moved out to the edge of the board sidewalk and stood there, sucking uselessly on a cigarette gone dead. He swung his head to follow the diminishing scuffing of Lilavelt's run-over boot heels. Luke Lilavelt was a man abnormally long between ankle and knee and he walked with a queer, high-kneed shuffling. He appeared constantly on the verge of stumbling, but he never did. The man, thought Wall morosely, was completely unlovely any way you looked at him, but he held the power and he snapped the whip. Wall spun his cigarette into the pale, starlit dust of the street and turned uptown.

It was fairly late but the lights were still on in Reed Howell's eating house and Wall, realizing abruptly that he'd had no food for upward of eight hours, turned in there. Reed Howell's greeting was casual but remote and with no real friendliness, and this, mused Dave Wall bleakly, was just another example of the stigma his association with Luke Lilavelt inflicted. He ate with silent hunger, though without relish.

How long since the simple savors of life had been his? It seemed an eternity, while actually measuring the better part of four years. Luke Lilavelt had also done that to him, robbing him of the friendship of decent men, pushing him into a world of half light. He had forgotten how to

13

laugh with real enjoyment because there was no one to laugh with him; he had become an automaton that went through the motions, no more. He functioned, but he did not live. The things that counted seemed to have dried up inside him, leaving him only a husk.

He finished his supper, paid for it, built a cigarette, and then with something almost wistful in his manner paused, hoping for some word of friendliness from Reed Howell. But none came, and, as he moved to the door, he said: "Good night, Reed."

Howell's answering—"Good night."—was purely automatic and held nothing at all, closing Wall out completely, and Wall, as he stepped into the outer darkness, wondered if he looked as furtive as he felt.

This town of Basin had once been Dave Wall's town and he could, in those days, count a friend behind every door. Now, although every black-shadowed angle and starlit roof line was familiar, he felt the outcast, the pariah. It was impossible not to know revolt over this, even though he knew the fault was his own. His mood was darker than usual when he pushed through the swinging half doors of Mize Callan's Empire House.

Callan was behind the bar, shaking dice with Pat Shea and Hub Lisenbee. A solo game was going on at a corner table and Oren White, dealing, looked up and went completely still, a card in suspended motion between his fingers. It was a deliberate thing, done deliberately by White to draw the attention of the other players to Dave Wall's presence, and Wall, seeing and understanding it as such, knew a surging gust of cold anger. He half whirled and started for White, his voice lashing out ahead of him.

"Go on . . . go on. Finish the deal, damn you."

Mize Callan's heavy growl was an echo to Wall's words. "That'll be all, Dave. Let it lay."

Wall stopped, looked at Callan. The saloon owner held a dice box in his left hand, but his right was out of sight under the bar. Callan's broad, veined face was expressionless, but his eyes were not. They were cold, challenging, unwavering.

Wall had rolled up on his toes, like something ready to leap, or a spring tensed to uncoil violently. Fat Hub Lisenbee swallowed heavily, licked his lips, and began to sidle along the bar front, out of the line of fire.

Then Wall shook his head as though to clear it and sagged back on his heels. "All right, Mize," he mumbled wearily, "all right." He turned and went back through the doors.

Damn them . . . damn them all! They might treat him as if he were a mangy dog, but there wasn't one of them who had the nerve to fight Luke Lilavelt openly. And what did they know about how his own hands were tied?

For a moment Wall played with the thought of heading out to the Connell Ranch to see Judith and Jerry and the kids, but then he knew there would be no profit in this, either; it would only make more difficult his leaving for the Crimson Hills. The thing to do in his present mood was get out of town, out into the desert, and know a few hours of peace even at the cost of his ever-deepening loneliness of spirit. He went down to Hub Lisenbee's stable, where he'd left his horses.

The stable was dark but it was a familiar place and he had no trouble in locating his gear, saddling up, and setting the pack. He added half a sack of oats to the pack horse's load, and when he rode out of town, he cast no backward look.

The stars were high and bright, and black shadows flowed along under him and the animals as they moved down the long slope into the desert and headed due north, where, a round hundred miles distant, lay Luke Lilavelt's Crimson Hills range. A year before Wall had made this same trip and, knowing what lay ahead, realized there could be no hurry, so he let the horses find their own settled, jogging, long-travel pace.

Ahead the desert ran out its distance under the stars and lost itself in far darkness. It had its own character, this land had, and its own breath that was a compound of silence, space, and the flavor of sage's pungency.

Wall had made many such long and lonely trips

to various holdings in the interests of Luke Lilavelt and knew how to achieve the locked-away stoicism to carry through the slow hours and long miles. He rode this night out and reached the first water hole along the trail just as gray dawn began fading out the stars. He made a frugal camp, unsaddled, watered and grained the horses. He built a minute fire of dead sage roots, cooked coffee and bacon, had a smoke, then crawled into the lee of a clump of sage, and slept until the prying heat of a climbing sun reached and woke him. Again he saddled and packed and moved on.

Recalling his first trip to the Crimson Hills, he knew that this would be an empty, lonely, weary day, just the desert and his thoughts. Time and the steady slogging pace of the horses would take care of the first and, no matter how they ran, he would have to bear with the latter. For, however far and long a man rode, he could never get away from himself.

The sun climbed to its zenith and laid a harsh and powerful touch across an empty world. Sweat started and ran and dried, leaving a crusted rime on the hides of the horses and the salt of its bitterness stung a man's eyes and his lips. The desert's bleached and unceasing glare beat at a man's eyes and pinched them down to narrowed slits and the heat was a baking weight across his shoulders. By midafternoon all spring had gone from the horses' stride and the first blue and welcome tide of dusk found them completely jaded. But Wall kept them to it, aiming for a certain dry wash he remembered, where, beneath a high cutbank, a small and brackish water hole lay.

Coming in on the place, the slow plod of the horses muffled by the reddish sandy earth, Wall abruptly straightened in the saddle, for the still air now held the dry pungency of wood smoke, and then Wall, peering ahead, picked up the faint reflected radiance of the fire. Instantly Wall pushed aside the torpor that the long and lonely ride had settled on him, and he rode, high and alert, as his horses slid down a bank into the dry wash and their hoofs rang loudly on the bleached and alkali-whitened cobbles of its bed. Now Wall saw the fire clearly and he saw the two figures, that had been hunkered beside it, straighten up and drift swiftly beyond the reach of its thin glow.

Wall sent in his hail. "Hello . . . the fire!"

There was a long moment of silence before the surly reply came. "Keep on driftin'. This camp is taken!"

Realizing that mounted, he made a solid outline against the fading sky, Wall went swiftly from his saddle and then, past the bulk of his horse, laid down his purpose, flatly harsh and with no compromise. "This is the only water within miles and it's free. I'm coming in!"

The horses smelled the water and were eager for it. They needed no urging to move up and Wall still used the shelter of their bulk as he moved in. He stopped just beyond the reach of the fire glow. "Well?"

Moving in, he had marked things as best he could and he felt he had those two slinking figures pretty well placed, so now he put the pressure of decision on them. It was his way, the combination of recklessness, stubborn courage, and a harsh knowledge of men gleaned down through some rough and perilous years. He waited them out, alert for anything, while the tension built up. One of them weakened under it.

"Who are you?"

"That doesn't matter. I need this water and I'm throwing off here. Your move!"

There it was again. That pressure—direct, grim, unrelenting. They began to hedge.

"There's more water, five miles west along this wash."

"Not interested," rapped Wall. "You can head for it if you don't like my company. Here is where I stop."

There was a stir of movement farther along the wash and a slim figure in jeans and jumper came out of the shadows and up to the fire and a girl's fresh voice rang clearly.

"If there's any single call on this camp, it's

mine. For I was here first. And I say you are welcome, friend."

Dave Wall went very still for one sharp moment, wondering if the day's long ride under the desert sun had addled him and was making him see and hear things that were pure fancy and without any real substance? For her face was clear in the firelight and memory struck strongly at Wall.

It reached back to his former trip to the Crimson Hills headquarters. He had been returning then, and to avoid the hard ride across the desert had swung west and south by way of Crater City. She had been riding out of Crater City when Wall rode in. She had passed so close to him as to leave a faint and haunting fragrance, along with the memory of a loveliness as bright and clear and clean as morning sunshine.

There had never been any sane reason, Wall knew, why his memory of her had remained so strong and vividly with him, for he had no idea who she was and his chance of ever seeing her again had been virtually non-existent. And even if there could have been, there would be no meaning to it. For the distance between the poles of the earth was no greater than the gulf that must exist between such a girl and him, Dave Wall, trouble-shooter for most of Luke Lilavelt's worst range piracies. Yet, in a miasma of dark and somber thoughts, the one of her had remained bright and untarnished and more than once had helped Dave Wall through his blacker moods.

Now, here she was, right in front of him again. There could be no mistake. It was the same girl, the one of that single, bright memory. Then she had been in divided skirt and blouse. Now she wore a more severely practical garb for saddle work. But all the shining loveliness was there, as before. Her sleek, bright head was high and erect with pride and spirit, but despite the ruddy glow of the fire it struck Dave Wall that there was strain and pallor in her face.

He could not have been more astounded had a star fallen at his feet and the wonder of it held him long silent. But he found his voice at last. "Obliged, ma'am. I guess that settles the argument." He swung his head and his voice was a hard lash. "Come in to the fire, you two . . . where I can see you better. Move!" Wall drew a gun as he spoke. There was something about this set-up that wasn't right, wasn't regular, and the prescience of this was rubbing across his nerve ends, sharpening them. "Move!" he snapped again.

The renewed build-up of pressure was too much for the skulkers. They came in to the firelight, full of a sullen furtiveness. At his first clear glance, Wall knew the type. Riff-raff of the cattle country. Drifters. Grub-line riders. Picking up a few days of work here, a few more there.

21

Nothing solid or steady about them and not above crime of any sort if they thought they could get away with it.

"Your trail manners are rotten," said Wall bluntly. "Just why should you object to my sharing this camp?"

Now it was the girl who said a startling thing. "Ask them also why they rummaged my saddlebags and took my gun?"

One of the drifters swung his head, soundlessly snarling. He jumped a foot as Dave Wall's gun spat hard thunder and a slug lashed the ground beside him. Before the echoes could come back, Wall growled: "Careful! Watch yourselves! Turn around!"

The heavy-set one of the two showed a brief flare of truculence. "Mister, you take in too much trail. You . . ."

"Turn around!"

It came out of Dave Wall like an invisible tide, a breath of wicked ruthlessness. The drifters turned jerkily. Wall took their guns, then turned to the girl. "Which one took your gun?'

"The heavy one. He put it inside his shirt."

With his free hand, Wall swung the fellow to face him. Wall saw the bulge of the gun, tucked in the waistband of the drifter's jeans, under his shirt. With a sweep of his hand Wall ripped the shirt from grimy collar to waist. He lifted away the gun, a light-calibered, slim-barreled weapon.

Wall was thinking: *This girl, in a wide and lonely land. And two slimy ones like these. And they had taken away her only means of protecting herself.* Wall's eyes went very cold. "There's a special hell reserved for whelps like you two. I've a notion to send you there, now." He lifted his voice. "Have they got saddle guns, ma'am?"

"I don't know. I'll see." The girl darted off into the dark, and Wall heard the weary stirring and trampling of horses. The girl came back. "No saddle guns."

"Good enough." Wall jerked his head. "Get! You two are riding. You can hunt that other water hole you spoke of."

The heavy-set drifter leered. "That'll make it chummy for you and . . ."

Wall hit him before he could get out further words, hit him savagely, full across the face with the flat of his gun, knocking the fellow sprawling, where he lay sniffling blood through a broken nose, dazed and half stunned. A raging, deadly note came into Wall's voice. "The pair of you have exactly two minutes to get out of here. You better believe I mean that."

The second of the two, lank and gangling, evidently believed Wall, for he dragged his bleeding companion to his feet and hurried him, stumbling and lurching, out into the darkness, with Wall following closely.

There were three horses and one of them limped

badly as it moved a trifle apart. "Mine," said the girl at Wall's elbow. "And the reason I'm not home by this time."

The lanky drifter boosted his partner into the saddle, swung up on his own horse. Dave Wall gave his final harsh warning. "Ride far!"

The horses clattered away up the wash and Wall listened until the sound of their going had faded out. Then he turned to the girl and his tone was still slightly rough from the residue of his mood.

"Day or night, even with a sound horse under you, this is no country for a girl like you to be riding alone."

She tossed her head. "I've ridden it all my life. I'd been visiting friends over at Cottonwood off the east edge of the desert and I was taking a short cut home. When my horse, sliding down a cutbank, went lame, I headed for the nearest water, which was here. It was one of those things that might never happen again."

"Yet it did happen, and the consequences could have been . . . unpleasant. Any idea who that worthless pair are?"

"No. Probably a couple of Window Sash hands. They're the type Luke Lilavelt likes on his payroll, so I've heard. No decent person would ever ride for Lilavelt."

The darkness hid the ironic bitterness that pulled at Dave Wall's lips. He was in no position to argue the point. He went back to the fire to unsaddle swiftly and unpack, watering his horses, then graining them. He broke out his frugal camp outfit, looked at the girl.

"You had any supper?"

She hesitated, started to shake her head, then said quickly: "It doesn't matter. As I said, I expected to be home by this time."

"Only you're not," said Wall brusquely. "You're here and you've had no supper and you're hungry. I've enough for two."

He stirred up the fire and got to work. Beyond the flames the girl sat cross-legged, watching him. Soon the savoriness of frying bacon and steaming coffee flavored the night air. Wall did not miss the unconscious intentness and eagerness of the girl's manner.

"How long have you been here?" he asked abruptly.

"Since sunup this morning. I much prefer to ride the desert at night. I left Cottonwood last evening. I knew that Dad expected me home by tonight. But when my horse went lame, there was nothing else I could do but make for the nearest water and wait for Dad and the boys to come looking for me. They're sure to try this water hole. So, I had nothing to worry about until . . . until those two came riding in. As soon as I saw the type they were, I thought I'd better get my gun out of my saddlebags. But they guessed what

I was after and that . . . that big brute got there first. Right after that you rode in."

She wasn't, Wall realized, entirely at ease, even now. She had courage, this girl, but the experience had unsettled her and she couldn't hide all her feelings, despite her brave front. He handed her a plate of food and a cup of coffee.

"No more pretense," he said gruffly. "You're half starved and I know it. Get outside of that and you'll feel better. You've nothing to worry about now. Soon as we finish eating, I'll bring your bronc' up to the fire and have a look at it. If there's no chance of using the animal, I'll put your saddle on my pack horse, split up the pack, and hit the trail again in a couple of hours. Where's your home?"

"At Sweet Winds. I'm Tracy Sutton."

Wall lowered his head slightly to shadow his startled eyes. Surprises came fast this night, it seemed. This girl . . . Tracy Sutton. He'd heard that Bart Sutton had a daughter. And Sweet Winds was the name of Sutton's ranch headquarters.

"And I'd like," continued the girl after a slight pause, "to know the name of my benefactor. Or is that wish out of order?"

Dave Wall drew a deep breath, masked his face to inscrutability, and looked at her, wondering if it would mean anything to her. "Wall is the name . . . Dave Wall."

It meant something, all right. He saw her

start, saw her eyes widen, saw her even recoil slightly.

"Not . . . not Luke Lilavelt's man?" she stammered. "Not that . . . Dave Wall?" She spoke it as though naming the devil himself.

"I'm sorry," said Wall wearily, "but it is . . . that one."

Chapter Two

When Dave Wall had taken Tracy Sutton's gun from the burly drifter and returned it to her, she had tucked it from sight under her jumper. Now her hand stole toward it.

"No need of that," said Wall harshly. "You're as safe here as if you were in your own home. You should know that. I'm no ogre."

"From . . . from all that I've heard I could believe that you are," retorted the girl. "I've heard terrible things of you."

Wall laughed mirthlessly. "Probably. A man in my place has many things told about him, a great many of them lies. And even the truthful things are seldom improved in the telling. Now you've the evidence of your own eyes. Maybe if you trust them, you'll hit closer to the truth than you know."

Her eyes were accusing, her thoughts traveling their own line. "You're heading for Luke Lilavelt's Crimson Hills headquarters. Yes, that's where you're heading." Her lips scarcely moved and her voice was very low. It was as though she were thinking aloud. "Yes, you're heading for the Crimson Hills. That means trouble . . . for Dad. I've heard him say so, more than once. That the day Dave Wall rode into Crimson Hills, it would mean the start of a showdown between himself and Luke Lilavelt. It never seemed real to me. I never thought it would happen. But it has. You're here. You . . . Dave Wall."

Wall writhed inwardly at the way she looked at him. He knew that along the back trail, in his service of Luke Lilavelt, he'd left hatreds that would never die. To some extent he'd managed to shake off the regrets. It was all a part of the price he had to pay for doing the thing he'd set himself to do. To that realization he had hardened himself. But he never could harden himself to the aversion he now saw growing in this girl's clear eyes. Particularly this girl. It was like being whipped with a lash of fire. He broke silence on things he had virtually sworn to himself never to explain to anyone.

"There may be things you don't understand," he blurted huskily. "There are such things. Sometimes a man can't help himself. Sometimes he must do things under the whip of his own conscience and sense of honor. Sometimes he does things because the happiness and welfare of someone near and dear to him mean much more to him than does his own."

All of which made no impression whatever on Tracy Sutton. She was as distant as the stars. "Where," she asked coldly, "can there be any conscience or sense of honor in doing Luke Lilavelt's dirty work? Or does he pay you so much money nothing else matters?" Her hand had been stealing under her jumper again. Now it flicked out, gripping that slim-nosed gun. The muzzle dropped in line with Dave Wall's heart. "I could kill you," she said steadily, "and no one would ever blame me."

Wall had quieted, ironing back the gust of feeling that had swayed him. Now he was still and inscrutable again, his voice dryly impersonal.

"That's right, you could. You could say that I rode into your camp and that you had to shoot me for any one of a hundred reasons you might cook up, any of which would be accepted as gospel and legitimate by plenty of people. All of which would dispose of Dave Wall very satisfactorily, but it still wouldn't stop Luke Lilavelt from having his try at the Square S holdings . . . your father's ranch. Somewhere, somehow, Lilavelt would pick up another Dave Wall under another name. Probably he'd have to buy this new one with that big money you mentioned. Which would hurt his miserly soul, of course, but which he'd do if he had to. And then you probably wouldn't be lucky enough to have a chance to shoot that one, out here in the desert."

His glance was direct, taciturn, and telling nothing. She met it for a long moment, then color stole across her face and her hand and the gun in it fell to her side. Wall stood up and walked away.

He was soon back, leading the girl's crippled

mount. He had only to look, to feel the flinching quiver of that bad leg under gently kneading fingertips to know that here was a pony that would not be carrying a rider again for some time. By itself the horse could shuffle along after a fashion. But the weight of a saddle and rider would have the animal completely broken down inside a mile or two.

While he worked with the horse, Wall could feel the girl's guarded glance. She had put away her gun. Wall had known that she would, known that her entire gesture with the weapon had been merely thought with never any real intent. But there was no comfort in that, either. For in their own way, thoughts could wound as deeply as direct action.

Wall straightened up. "Out of the question to think of riding this horse. We'll ride my two and let this one follow along at its own speed. And we might as well start now as later."

He brought in his own horses, still weary, but stronger for water and grain. He cinched the girl's saddle on the pack horse, split up his gear as compactly as he could. He slung the sawbuck pack saddle up behind the cantle of his own. The girl hung back in the shadows, for the fire was guttering out. "I can stay here," she said. "Dad and the boys are sure to be along after a while."

"Maybe," said Wall briefly. "Maybe not until tomorrow. In the meantime a certain pair of two-legged coyotes might still be prowling. Don't be so proud and stubborn. Get in your saddle and come along. A little more of my enforced company won't contaminate you any worse than it already has."

That brought a flare from her. "Am I to be blamed for . . . for wondering about you? After all . . ."

"The only thing you could be blamed for," cut in Wall, "is being foolish enough to think that I'd leave you here alone. You'll make it easier for both of us if you'll scramble into that saddle and quit arguing."

He built a cigarette, scratched a match, and cupped it briefly before his face. The light of it turned his weather-darkened features into a hard and settled mask of dull bronze. The girl, watching, caught the line of his profile and she knew that here, regardless of what else he might be, was no man of weakness. There was a stony will in him that it was useless to fight. Wall heard the saddle girth creak as the girl put her weight into the stirrup. So then he mounted and rode away to the north without looking back.

For some distance Tracy Sutton trailed behind, then finally moved up even with him. "That way lies home," she said stiffly, pointing more to the west.

"Fair enough," murmured Wall. "Lead on."

After that silence held between them while the

miles and the hours ran out. The girl neither spoke nor looked at Wall and against the stars her shoulders showed a straight, uncompromising set. The pace was steady but not fast, and Wall, thinking of the crippled horse following, held it so. From time to time he turned his head, listening until he heard the uneven, broken cadence of the animal's stride. Once, when he wasn't certain, he pulled almost to a stop, and then the girl turned almost impatiently.

"You don't need to hold down the pace on my account," she said tartly.

"Wasn't thinking of that at all," answered Wall dryly. "But there's a faithful little bronc' with a very bad leg trying to keep up back there."

Instantly he knew the girl was contrite and her voice sounded slightly muffled. "You make me ashamed. I . . . I wasn't thinking . . ."

"Sure," said Wall gently. "I knew that."

Tracy Sutton stared ahead into the night, trying to figure out this man. There was much that she did not know about men and their ways, about the things that made them what they were. At home, under the powerful shelter of her father's affection and authority, surrounded by the loyalty of a sound and steady crew who were proud of her and slaves to her every wish and whim, she had been long shielded from the rougher aspects of the sex. She had been privileged to ride this country freely and as far as she wished because she was Bart Sutton's daughter. And never before until this night had she actually come face to face with the ugliness that had reared its head when those two drifters had moved in on her camp at the dry wash water hole.

Honest with herself, she knew she had been desperately frightened, though her pride would not allow her to show it openly. And she thought now of the tremendous relief she had known when this Dave Wall had ridden in through the dusk and laid down his hard and uncompromising challenge to the two drifters. Never had the presence of another human being been more welcome.

She recalled the almost contemptuous ease with which he'd brought the two drifters to heel and that brief moment of explosive savagery he'd shown when he'd smashed the flat of his gun into the face of the burly renegade in retaliation for an uncouth remark.

She hadn't known then who he was—hadn't known that this was Dave Wall—*the* Dave Wall. The man who did Luke Lilavelt's dirty work, the man who made Luke Lilavelt's most bare-faced and shameless range piracies go. All she knew at the moment was that he was a big, dark figure of a man who carried something about him that made a pair of drifting renegades cringe and crawl.

But now she knew who he was, and why he was

here. For she'd heard her father say more than once that when Dave Wall—*the* Dave Wall—rode into the Crimson Hills outfit, then battle, savage and without quarter, loomed ahead.

Tracy Sutton thought of how she had put her gun on him and her cheeks burned with the embarrassment of such a childish, senselessly melodramatic move. Dave Wall had virtually ignored the move, which was what it deserved, and had then gone about making preparations to get her safely home, paying no attention at all to any objections she raised.

She turned her head slightly, looking at him guardedly. It was too dark to make out any detail. Just a big dark figure of a man, in the saddle now instead of afoot, holding down the pace so that a lamed horse could keep up. That was what she couldn't figure. For, when he'd clubbed down the burly drifter with his gun, she had somehow gotten the impression that here was a man with little consideration or faith in most other humans and none at all in some of them. Yet he had remembered a lamed horse where she had partially forgotten. . . .

It was nearing midnight when Tracy Sutton reined in abruptly and stood high in her stirrups to listen. Dave Wall, pulling in beside her, drawled: "Yeah . . . that's right. Hoofs out ahead. Maybe half a dozen riders. Probably your people out looking for you. Better give them a call."

Tracy did so, her clear young voice carrying across the night. There came a gruff answering shout reflecting a solid gladness and relief. The rumble of hoofs deepened and swelled, rolling down upon them, and then the massed bulk of several riders loomed in the thin star glow.

"Over here, Dad!" called the girl, and then she moved out to meet them. Dave Wall thumbed out his smoking, rolled, and lit one, casual and relaxed in his saddle, yet thinly alert.

A deep voice boomed. "Tracy! Child, you've had me devilishly worried. You should have been home by sundown. What happened?"

Wall could hear the girl explaining briefly. "I think those two drifters might have grown very unpleasant if Dave Wall hadn't happened along to drive them off."

"Girl," rumbled that deep voice, "did I hear you right? Did you say . . . Dave Wall?"

"That's right, Dad. *The* Dave Wall, too. Come over here and meet him. But remember, he's been very decent and thoughtful. As I told you, he drove those two drifters off. Then he shared his supper with me, loaned me his pack horse to ride, and was bringing me home. It was the kind of treatment I didn't expect after all the things I've heard said about him. Which shows how unfair talk can be, sometimes."

This brought a harsh and cynical growl. "We'll see about that."

The dark blot of riders spread and thinned, half encircling Wall as they moved in on him. Bart Sutton, a thick and dominant figure against the stars, faced Dave Wall, and his heavy voice was full of pushing suspicion and hostility.

"That's correct, what Tracy just told me? You're Lilavelt's main trouble-shooter . . . Dave Wall?"

"Some call me that," acknowledged Wall bleakly.

Bart Sutton seemed to tower even more massively in his saddle. "It seems you've done my daughter a kindness. Why?"

Wall took a final drag of his cigarette, crushed out the butt on his saddle horn with a hard irritability. "I'll let you guess at that, if you're too narrow between the ears to understand. And tell these hands of yours to give back a little . . . I don't like to be crowded."

One of Sutton's riders spoke wickedly. "Proud rooster, ain't he? What for, I wonder?"

Wall spun his horse straight at the speaker. "Big bunch always makes for a big mouth," he rapped. "Come out of the gather and find out, friend."

"Hold it . . . hold it," rumbled Sutton. "Spike, mind your jaw. I'll handle this. Wall, we could ride you down."

"Maybe. But the rumpus would be considerable. Now I've still got country to cover. I'll take my pack horse, if it's all the same to you. The young lady shouldn't need it any more."

"Dad," said the girl, "we're not behaving very well, are we?"

"Coming to that," said Bart Sutton, his heavy tone slightly milder. "Wall, for the kindness you've done my daughter, I thank you. But I'm warning you . . . for the purpose you came into this country, I shall probably kill you."

"That," said Wall, dryly bleak, "may be."

Bart Sutton turned to his men, issuing curt orders. "Sandy, let Tracy have your horse. Spike, that's a stout bronco you ride and can carry double. You take Sandy with you, drift back, and pick up that lame horse and bring it in at its own gait."

Sutton swung down and swiftly stripped the girl's riding gear off Dave Wall's pack horse and handed it up to another rider to carry. Wall, content now that hostility for the moment was over with, dismounted and cinched the sawbuck saddle in place on his pack horse, and then deftly slung his gear. For a moment or two deep anger had burned in him, but it was now replaced with a sardonic, mirthless amusement.

What right had he to expect anything more than had been shown him? After all he was who he was—Dave Wall, trouble-shooter for Luke Lilavelt, whose mean and rapacious mind was dedicated to the proposition of bringing wreck and ruin to Bart Sutton and all he possessed. All of which Bart Sutton well knew and was entitled to resist by any and every means. As for gratitude for small favors done, ran Wall's cynical thought, how much real gratitude ever did exist in people? Damn little, if past experience meant anything.

And then he was completely startled. For Tracy Sutton was at his elbow, her hand on his arm. "I shall probably end up despising you," she said simply. "But at this moment I am truly grateful. Thank you, Dave Wall."

Before Wall could think of an answer, she had turned swiftly away and rose into her saddle. Bart Sutton growled an order and the mounted group spurred off into the night. Dave Wall found himself alone. It was, he thought bleakly, indicative. A man in his circumstance must always be alone.

The desert was gone, miles back. Here was a vast, slow-climbing sweep of country, bulwarked finally by tumbled hills. The Window Sash headquarters lay in an oblong basin in these Crimson Hills. Dave Wall rode up to the layout through the forming heat of midmorning.

There was nothing elaborate about the place. It was a typical Window Sash layout, reflecting Luke Lilavelt's reluctance to spend a dollar more than was absolutely necessary to get what he wanted from a headquarters, which was a crude, frugal, comfortless efficiency. There were three main buildings, a cabin, a bunkhouse, a cook shack. Besides a spread of corrals, a short line of feed sheds, these were all. Raw-boarded, unpainted, weather-beaten, just an ugly minimum where men might live and carry out Luke Lilavelt's orders.

The place seemed deserted until, in the doorway of the cook shack, a grossly fat man appeared, stripped to the waist, a dirty flour sack tied as an apron about his bulging middle. His shapeless torso and moon face glistened with sweat. He watched Wall's approach with little, pale eyes that seemed to peep slyly past rolls of fat.

Wall jerked a brief nod. "Tom Burke . . . where is he?"

The fat man gave Wall a careful visual going over before he answered with a moist meatiness. "Out. He'll be back directly. You're Wall?"

Wall's eyes narrowed. "That's right. How'd you know?"

The fat man shrugged. "Made a guess. You'll be hungry. Come on in."

Wall unsaddled, stacked his gear, and turned his weary horses into the corral. In the cook shack the fat man had steak and potatoes and coffee waiting for him. It was good food, well cooked. The fat man knew his business and, for all his bulk, moved about with a disconcerting lightness and sureness. Wall had just finished eating when hoofs rattled outside.

"There's Burke and the crew," said the cook.

Dave Wall knew Tom Burke, but the rest of the crew were strangers to him. Burke was solidly built, ruddy, and square of jaw. He made no move toward shaking hands, and he spoke with a low curtness. "I can guess what this means, Wall."

Wall said: "Here's the authority. Sorry, Burke."

Burke read Lilavelt's note, tore it to bits, and let the pieces fritter through loose fingers. "You needn't be. I'm not. Come on over to the cabin and I'll hand the tally books and other ranch records to you."

The cabin was small, not over ten by ten, just large enough for a couple of wall bunks, a table, and a couple of chairs. Burke had kept it reasonably tidy. He pulled a box from under one of the bunks and put it on the table.

"All the records are in here. Want me to go over them with you?"

Wall shook his head. "Checking records is not what I'm here for. If you say they're right, that's good enough for me."

Burke sat on a bunk, brought out his war bag, and began packing it. "Been waiting for an excuse to do this. My chance to break with Lilavelt. A man can stomach just so much and I'm 'way past my limit. I make no claim toward sprouting wings, but working for Luke Lilavelt makes a dog out of a man. I don't like the feeling."

Burke's head came up and he looked defiantly at Wall as he said this, as though half expecting Wall to challenge the statement. Quietly Wall said: "You can call Lilavelt anything you want and it's all right with me."

Burke jammed a spare shirt into his war bag with unnecessary vehemence. "I don't understand you, Wall. I swear I don't. Anybody who takes the trouble to look close can see a streak of decency in you a mile wide. Yet every chunk of dirty business that Luke Lilavelt can dig up and wants hatched out for him, you take hold of and put across. Maybe big money has wider limits for you than for me. But I don't think it's that entirely, either, for there's no look of money greed about you. Just what is the answer?"

Wall shook his head. "My own. One of those things."

"I'm not the smartest man in the world by a hell of a lot," went on Burke. "But neither am I the biggest damn' fool. You're not here to take over because I've failed to run this headquarters at a profit for Lilavelt. You're here to start putting the pressure on Bart Sutton. Lilavelt is reaching out those damn' dirty claws of his again at a better man. It's a chore I wouldn't touch, for Bart Sutton is a damn' fine man. I'm glad I'm leaving. I hope

Sutton whips hell out of you and Lilavelt both, Wall."

Again Burke's head came up with that look of defiance.

Wall showed a small, weary, mirthless smile. "Always did admire a man with the guts to speak his real feelings, Tom. Suppose we let it lay that way. How does the crew shape up?"

"Tres Debley is the lone one of them who could ride for me if I owned this spread. The rest aren't worth hell room, but they're the sort to come in handy in putting the skids under Bart Sutton. I say again, I like Bart Sutton. He's a white man . . . one of the best. I hope he turns out to be the mouthful that Luke Lilavelt chokes to death on."

Tom Burke shouldered his war bag, lifted down a scabbarded carbine from a wall peg, turned to the door, and paused there. He laid a long, intent glance on Dave Wall, then spoke gruffly.

"There's a part of you, Wall, that makes me want to shake hands with you. There's another part that won't let me. But I'll say this last thing. Lilavelt has a spy planted in this outfit. Don't let that cook, Hippo Dell, fool you. He looks dumb, but he's not. He looks like a big, soft toad, but he's the strongest man I ever saw and one of the wickedest in a fight. When you tangle with Hippo, as you probably will, that will be one time when I wish you luck. You'll need it. *Adiós.*"

Wall stood in the cabin doorway, watching Tom Burke ride off. Soundlessly Wall murmured: *I envy you, Tom Burke. You can ride away, make a clean break. Yeah, I envy you.*

This mood held until Burke was out of sight. Then Wall shook himself and the old cloak of dark inscrutability came back and he headed over to the bunkhouse where he knew the crew had gathered, waiting for him to show. They looked him over guardedly and Wall, filling the doorway of the place, gave them back a measuring stare. He spoke curtly.

"There's been a change in bosses. I'm the new one. The name is Dave Wall. Any questions?"

A thin and spidery rider with a strangely small round head thickly matted with tightly curled black hair spoke waspishly. "Yeah. How much longer do we have to walk around Bart Sutton like he was God? How much longer do we have to go on ridin' six or seven miles out of our way to get to Crater City, instead of short-cuttin' it across Square S range? Me, I'm plenty sick of that kind of jackass business."

"That's right," agreed another rider. "As it stands, we've had to swing plumb to the north around Sutton's headquarters and then cut back south across the big lava rim to get to town. And there's no sense to it."

"Sutton objects to us crossing his range, then?" said Wall.

"Yeah, he does. And Burke didn't have the nerve to tell him where to go."

"Tom Burke," said Wall coldly, "never lacked for nerve or common sense, either. Until I say different, we'll still take the long way around to Crater City."

There was a rider sitting on one of the bunks, his hat beside him, who had been staring unwinkingly at Wall. He was burly, powerful, with eyes so pale they seemed almost milky blue. His hair, straw-colored and coarse, was close-cropped and stood up like a roach. Now he spat and cursed.

"When in hell," he wanted to know, "is Lilavelt going to send a real fightin' man to boss this spread?"

"That," chimed in the spidery, round-headed one, "is what I want to know, too, Whitey."

Here it was again, thought Dave Wall bleakly, part of the never-changing pattern. A pattern he'd met up with several times before in some of Lilavelt's hard-boiled outfits he'd been sent to take charge of. There was always some doubter who liked his own fighting ability and was anxious to prove it, always someone anxious to test the legend of Dave Wall and prove it a myth. You didn't try and reason with one of that sort; palaver of any sort would be mistaken as weakness. With that sort there was only one way to convince. So now Dave Wall moved swiftly, wickedly ruthless.

In two steps he had moved before Whitey, who, startled, was lunging erect. Wall hit him on the jaw with a short, hooking punch and knocked him back across the bunk. But Whitey was tough, full of burly, animal resistance. He smacked into the side of the place, bounced back, rolled off the end of the bunk, and came up with a rush. He dove at Wall, getting partially under a punch that bounced off the top of his bristling head. He got both arms about Wall's body and pushed him backward.

Wall's hips hit the bunkhouse table, sending it skittering. Whitey swung Wall half around and pinned him between the ends of two of the bunks. Then he set about giving out with his dirtiest best. He brought a high, sharp heel stamping down on Wall's instep. He bunched a knee and brought it up savagely, again and again. He had his bristle head jammed hard against Wall's chest and he kept butting with it, jerking it up in short, battering drives under Wall's chin, snapping Wall's head back. Wall could feel the warm slime of blood begin to dribble down his lips.

Now Whitey whipped his right arm free and shot his hand up, feeling for Wall's face, fingers spread and stabbing, gouging at Wall's eyes. Every movement was furious, savage, fast, calculated to overwhelm and disable as quickly as possible. Wall twisted his hips, catching that

46

gouging knee against one thigh. He threw his left hand across his face to ward off Whitey's feral, clawing fingers. And then, with his clenched right fist, Wall began to hit short, grinding punches, clubbing Whitey on the temple. Whitey twisted his head sideways to try and shield his temple from those jarring, stunning blows that hurt savagely. Then Wall smashed him at the base of the skull and behind the ear.

Whitey couldn't stand this and began to pull away, and Wall, gaining a little room, dropped his right fist low, then brought it up viciously. He felt Whitey's mouth pulp under the impact. Hurt and shaken, Whitey broke completely clear, set himself, and aimed a heavy swing at Wall's face.

Whitey was better at crude rough-and-tumble than he was at swinging punches. He started this one too roundabout and swinging, and Dave Wall ducked Whitey's whistling fist, went in under it, and with full forward drive and rolling shoulder smashed rock-hard knuckles into Whitey's midriff. He could feel Whitey's belly muscles cave, and he knew this one had really hurt. Whitey's jaw dropped and he gasped with a groaning thickness. Wall swarmed in, making the most of his advantage.

He clipped Whitey's sagging jaw with a left and wrecked his lips still further with another driving right. Whitey reeled across the bunkhouse and now it was his turn to be cornered and pinned. And Wall kept him so with a succession of slashing punches.

Whitey's forte of rough-and-tumble, of butting, gouging, kneeing, and stomping was of no use to him now and this clean exchange of punches he did not understand. He pawed and swung clumsily, a little more weakly and blindly all the time. But Whitey was already a whipped man and it was just a question of how much more punishment Dave Wall wanted to hand out to make this lesson stick. He ended it finally with a jolting left and a thundering right to the angle of Whitey's wobbling jaw. Whitey went down, sick, bloody, retching, and thoroughly beaten.

Wall stepped back, spat out a mouthful of blood. At that moment a voice rapped curtly: "Don't try it, Nick . . . don't try it!"

Dave Wall came around, swaying. The spidery, round-headed rider had a gun half drawn, his face pulled and savage. But there was another rider, lean and brown and with sun-puckered eyes, whose gun was fully drawn and couched for business, and he said: "Whitey asked for that, Nick. Let go of your gun!"

Nick obeyed, grudgingly, like something poisonous drawing back into a hole after being on the very verge of striking. In his waspish way he droned: "I'll remember this, Debley . . . I surely will."

Wall scrubbed the back of a hand across his crimsoned lips. He lashed Nick with a glance that was all gray ice. "Now that I'm looking at you, you can try for your gun any time. Or don't you like an even break?"

Nick, it seemed, didn't. He snarled soundlessly, but made no move. Wall stepped forward and slapped Nick hard across the face with an open hand, knocking him back on a bunk. Wall waited, watching. But Nick took this, too. Only his eyes fought back, black and hard and venomous.

Wall looked at the rider who had held Nick off. "You're Tres Debley?"

"That's right."

"Obliged. When I'm not around, you're in charge." Wall's raking glance touched the rest. "Any more questions?"

He waited out a long silence, then looked at Whitey and Nick. "You two are through. Come over to the cabin and get your time."

Wall scrubbed his leaking lips again, turned, and stalked out, nearly bumping into the fat cook, Hippo Dell, who had evidently been drawn by the sounds of battle. Wall's temper still held a red-hot edge.

"Don't skulk," he rapped harshly. "If you wanted a front seat, why didn't you come in?"

Hippo's moon face was expressionless. He said moistly: "Nick Karnes and Whitey Brewer are good men, too good to fire just because they tested you out, Wall. No real harm done and you'll find it hard to replace . . ."

"They're fired," cut in Wall. "When I want your advice, Dell, I'll ask for it. That clear enough?"

Hippo's face remained a bland mask, but his little eyes burned. "That's clear," he admitted. Then he turned away, moving with that queer gait that was at once so ponderous, yet so deceptively light.

Wall went over to the cabin, found a tin basin and a bucket half full of water. His shirt was splotched with his own blood and that of Whitey Brewer's, so he took it off, washed up, rinsed his mouth out several times until the bleeding of his cut lips stopped, then dug a clean shirt out of his gear, and donned it. After which he made out Whitey Brewer's and Nick Karnes's time and was waiting at the cabin door when they came for it.

Whitey was still a thoroughly whipped man, his pale eyes still numb and slightly vacant from the beating he had taken and his face and mouth were dark with bruises and swollen grotesquely. He took his time and turned away without a word or show of feeling of any kind. At best, Whitey's wits were none too keen and just now they were sadly scrambled.

On the other hand, while Nick Karnes said nothing, he paused for a brief moment, staring at Dave Wall with a fixity that suggested he was getting the full of something that he was locking away for future reference. In that look was a threat, a malignant promise. Wall broke it up with harsh words.

"Get . . . you damned little snake!"

Still Nick did not speak, save for that same soundless snarl, and his eyes burned with that same dark threat as he followed Whitey over to the corrals.

Dave Wall watched until they rode away, then turned and went over to a bunk and stretched out, all the weariness of a sleepless previous night and a recent savage physical brawl pulling at him. The moment his eyes closed he was asleep.

Chapter Three

Dave Wall slept all afternoon, awoke just at sunset. He was rested, but stiff and sore from the brawl with Whitey Brewer. Another dousing of his bruised face and mouth in cold water cleared his head and he was fairly easy and relaxed when the supper gong rattled and he went over to the cook shack.

Here there was a definite uncertainty in the air, but also the grudging respect of hard men for one who had proven his toughness and ability and the right to run the show. Hippo Dell moved softly around, bland and expressionless, setting out the supper. He still was without a shirt, still sweating, and his blubbery torso shone greasily in the yellow lamp glow. Wall thought of how Tom Burke had described Dell—a big, soft slug, but bull strong. Part of the description, thought Wall, was apt enough. For the rest he'd have to guess.

Wall ran his glance around the table. "Debley I know. The rest of you name yourselves."

From left to right it ran Olds, Challis, Muir, and Caraway. Olds blurted: "Any objections to us riding into Crater City tonight, Wall?"

Wall shrugged. "Not in the least. Just so you're back ready and able to do a day's work tomorrow.

And see you don't cross any part of Square S range."

"You're the doctor," mumbled Challis, his jaws busy.

Supper over, Wall went back to the cabin, lit the lamp, and settled down to another evening of loneliness. This was another part of his life, it seemed, that had become a settled thing. Only tonight, for some reason, the loneliness was strangely irksome. For a long time now, Dave Wall had become used to his own company and he had the solitary man's ability to drop back into a stoic patience that shut out the passage of time. For one thing, bossing a tough crew on a tough layout, always called for holding yourself apart. To mix too much with such a crew during leisure hours was to invite familiarity and from there breakdown in authority was quick and sure. You handled a tough crew at arm's length, always. It was the only way to hold their doubtful respect.

But this, mused Wall bleakly, was no cure for the loneliness that grated on him this night. Perhaps it was so because he was remembering so clearly where he was and who he was with the previous night at this time.

Just about now Tracy Sutton out in the star-filled stillness of the desert had been watching him with a grave, accusing stillness, hating him, no doubt, because of who he was, and knowing that his arrival on this range boded no good for her father. Dave Wall, trouble-shooter for Luke Lilavelt. Dave Wall, moving always in the shadows of a dark reputation. Yet, even though she hated him, she had been there, across the fire from him, and secure because of his presence. Here was one comforting and satisfying thought, at least, to hang onto.

Wall sat with his somber thoughts in the warm stillness, a cigarette gone dead in his fingers, and he listened to the riders spurring out for Crater City. Renegades to some extent they might be, but they were richer than he. At least they had companionship other than their own nagging and useless thoughts.

The lamp guttered and flickered, for the wick needed trimming. At the cabin door a spur tinkled softly and Tres Debley said: "All right if I come in?"

Wall, liking this man, spoke quickly: "Sure . . . come on. Glad to have you. Anything in particular on your mind?"

"Yes and no." Debley sat on the edge of a bunk, built a smoke, staring soberly at the floor. There was a certain cleanness about Tres Debley that the other riders lacked. Not so much a physical thing, though he was clean-shaven, brown, and hard. Rather it was a certain streak of discernible character running through him. Now he spoke slowly.

"I pose as no saint. A man knocks around,

scrambles for three meals a day, a roof to throw his bedroll under, and a few dollars in his pocket. You accept your hire, do your job. Some jobs you come out of feeling clean. Others you feel . . . well, not so spotless. Even so, in time you forget. But for the job ahead, Wall, I don't know whether I'll be able to carry my weight. I thought I'd better tell you that."

Wall was watching Tres Debley closely. "And what job do you figure is ahead?"

"Why, rubbing out Bart Sutton. That's right, isn't it?" Tres Debley's head came up and he looked steadily at Wall.

Dave stirred restlessly. You couldn't lie to a man like this. Particularly because you liked him and because lying would have served no purpose anyhow. "That is putting it pretty bluntly," Dave Wall admitted slowly, "but it's just about what it amounts to."

Tres Debley nodded. "I figured so. And I don't like it. Wall, Bart Sutton is a hell of a good man. Oh, I've carried Luke Lilavelt's axe against other men, but most of them weren't a damned bit better in the early days than Lilavelt is now. They hogged range, pushed weaker men aside, or trampled them under, just like Lilavelt has done and is doing. They grew respectable only when they figured they had enough range and enough cows to do them the rest of their lives.

"But Bart Sutton ain't now and never was that

sort. He made his start on clear range. He never tried to walk on another man's neck or hog anything that didn't belong to him. He played a clean, straight game all the way. He took a bare chunk of bench land and made it into the finest damned ranch you ever saw. Ever been to the Square S headquarters?"

Wall shook his head. "No, I never have."

"Well, I was, once. I took a chance one day and dropped by the place. Nobody was home and I had a chance to look around. Sweet Winds, they call it. And rightly so. Up on that bench land there's always a breeze . . . a sweet one. You've smelled a wind coming in off some distant cedar slope? Kind of dry and fragrant? Well, that's the way it is up there. There's a grove of big sycamores, shading the ranch house. Bart Sutton planted those trees with his own hands. Everything is neat, well kept, well put together. Everything is clean, painted. It smacks of home and right living and good people.

"A girl lives there, Wall . . . Bart Sutton's girl. I saw her once, in Crater City. She's a clean strain, that girl . . . none finer. Pretty as a sunset. And . . . damn it all, maybe you don't understand, but this is one dirty job of Lilavelt's I want no part in. So, while it may sound queer for me to say I'd like to work under you, you're going to have to count me out. I'll take my time."

Dave Wall stared bleakly at the murky lamp.

"You're wrong, Tres. I do understand. That's the exquisite hell of it. I do understand. I'm not blaming you . . . and I don't want you to quit. You're the one man in this outfit I want to stay. If you will, I promise you I won't ask you to make one single move toward hurting Bart Sutton in any way."

Tres Debley jerked erect. "That don't make sense, man. If I ride for an outfit, then I ride with that outfit. No, that doesn't make sense."

"I know it doesn't," said Wall a trifle desperately. "But a break . . . there must be a break coming to me sometime. I've got to hang on to that hope or go completely crazy. If it doesn't come and the cards fall wrong, Tres, I'll let you know in time. Then you can quit. Fair enough?"

Tres Debley stared at Wall for a long time without answering. Then he nodded. "Fair enough. Most of us have reasons for what we do or don't do. Yours must be a good one."

Debley rose to leave. Wall got up, too, blew out the lamp. "How about showing me the usual route to town, Tres? I want to get these range limits fixed in my mind. And tonight there's a restlessness in me for some damned reason."

"Crater City it is," agreed Debley.

They took the long way around and from the upper slopes looked down on the lights of the Sutton headquarters as they passed. They saw the black cone of Crater Mountain, jutting against the stars to the west, and when they cut south to the lava rim that laid its dark barrier from Crater Mountain to the Crimson Hills, they saw below them, at the fringe of the desert gulf, the meager lights glittering that marked Crater City.

They dropped down the narrow trail that jackknifed across the face of the lava rim and the hoofs of their horses beat out a hard ringing on the solid rock. A quarter of a mile from the base of the rim and they were in Crater City, riding its single wide street, picking a hitch rail for their horses.

"I've no special purpose, now that we're here," said Wall quietly. "It was something to do."

"Sure"—nodded Tres Debley—"I know. We'll look around."

Dave Wall's first liking for this man deepened. There was depth and an instinct for understanding in Tres Debley.

They prowled the street. It wasn't much of a town, little more than a three-block length of scattered buildings. They paused before a general store, still open for trade. "I could stand some smoking," said Tres.

"And here," said Wall. "We'll split a caddy of Durham."

They went in and made their purchase from a lanky, bald-headed man. Hoofs beat out a muffled trumping along the street, came to a halt outside. Spurs clanked and Bart Sutton came in, accompanied by two riders. Under the lamplight the cattleman's hair showed a grizzling at the temples and his face looked like mahogany-tinted leather. His jaw was square and blunt and his wide-set eyes were cool and shrewd and direct. He was a man to approve at first glance.

Tres Debley said softly: "Bart Sutton, if you didn't know it, Wall."

One of the riders said something to Sutton who turned and looked over Wall and Debley with a measuring sternness. To the storekeeper he said: "Be with you in a minute, Tompkins." Then he came over to face Dave Wall.

"Last night I had no good look at your face, but I caught the set of your shoulders against the stars. You're Wall?"

"That's right," answered Wall quietly.

For a long moment their glances locked. Then Bart Sutton said: "I'll be riding over some of your Crimson Hills range tomorrow. You've probably figured out how simple it would be to run my Square S iron into a Window Sash. My men report some evidence of that already happening. I'm going to have a good look around, Wall."

"Fine," said Wall. "I'm interested, myself. So, I'll ride with you. Any critters we find with your brand so blotted, will be turned back to you. What time will you be passing by headquarters?"

Bart Sutton was plainly surprised. Here was quiet, affable reaction where he'd plainly expected hostility. "That," he admitted frankly, "I didn't figure on. Maybe it's a deep game you're playing, Wall?"

"Maybe. But brand blotting isn't part of it. I'll be looking for you, Mister Sutton."

"I'm not bluffing, Wall. I'll be there at sunup."

"Fine," said Wall again.

Again their glances locked and Bart Sutton's eyes pinched down in a slight puzzlement. Then he turned away and Wall and Tres Debley went out. They paused to stow their tobacco purchase away in their saddlebags. "He means it, Wall," said Debley. "He'll show up exactly when he says."

"That's what I want," said Wall. "Anything in the brand-blotting talk, Tres?"

Tres built a cigarette before answering slowly. "Afraid there is. Tom Burke never ordered it nor would he have stood for it on any open scale. But this is big range and broken, and those two you fired, Nick Karnes and Whitey Brewer . . . well . . ." Debley shrugged.

"Any others beside those two, Tres?"

"Not here, if that's what you mean." Debley's tone was flatly emphatic. "Strange as it may sound, coming from one working for a man like Luke Lilavelt, I want no part of that kind of business. I might steal a herd from some thief who stole them first, but I don't touch an honest man's cattle, not for myself or anybody else.

As for the rest of the crew, I wouldn't know."

"I was," said Wall, "speaking just of the rest of the crew. Present company completely excepted. Takes a mean man for a mean job, Tres."

Bart Sutton and his riders came out of the store, stood for a moment in conversation, after which the two hands went directly to their horses and rode out of town. But Sutton went along the street and turned in through swinging half doors under a faintly lit sign that proclaimed THE RIALTO.

"I've been wanting a chance for a good talk with Sutton," said Wall. "This looks like a good time."

"A talk with the enemy," murmured Tres Debley. "What's that mean, man . . . ultimatums, or things of that sort?"

"No. About a stretch of country, between the Monuments and Stinking Water. Whether it can't be opened to a trail herd without an argument."

"That's not what Luke Lilavelt wants," declared Debley, quickly shrewd. "He wants an argument, a fight, a hypocrite's cause to go after Sutton and wipe him out."

"Damn Lilavelt!" rapped Dave Wall harshly. "Damn him clear past hell!"

Tres Debley showed a small grin and dropped an approving hand on Wall's shoulder. "Go have your talk . . . and good luck. I'll meet you here in an hour. I see there's still a light in the kitchen of

Charlie Ring's hash house. Charlie and me rode together at one time. That was before his horse fell on him and broke him up so he couldn't ride any more. He likes me to drop in for a little chin-fest whenever I hit town."

Wall headed for The Rialto. This wish for a talk with Bart Sutton was no spur-of-the-moment idea. It had been at the back of his mind ever since leaving Luke Lilavelt's office back in Basin. Perhaps it was a product of wishful thinking, or a gnawing weariness of violence, a desire to arbitrate instead of fight. Maybe just to put off the inevitable for a time, while waiting for a break of some kind.

The winnowing doors of The Rialto gave under the pressure of his hand. Half through them he stopped dead still, a leaping alertness lifting him up on his toes, throwing his head and shoulders forward until the lights of the saloon carved his face into harsh bronze.

Fifteen feet from him stood Bart Sutton. The cattleman's back was to the door, his left elbow hooked on the bar, his right hand holding a glass with a short two fingers of whiskey half lifted to his lips. Sutton's entire attention was centered narrowly on Nick Karnes, who stood free of the bar, some two yards to Sutton's right side. Nick's feet were spread, he was in a weaving half crouch, and he had a gun drawn and pointing at the center of Bart Sutton's body.

Nick Karnes was drunk. It showed in the slight, slow weave of his shoulders, in the glazed hardness of his eyes, in the way he showed his teeth past thinned and twisted lips. Deadly drunk, oozing the same threat a poised rattlesnake might have—poised and ready to strike.

Farther along the bar, his back against it, thumbs hooked in his gun belt, was Whitey Brewer. Whitey's face was puffed all out of shape from the effect of Dave Wall's fists, and he held the same danger edge of liquor in him that Nick did. Whitey was watching the rest of the room, guarding Nick's back.

Nick Karnes was speaking, slowly and thickly. "Well . . . well, Sutton . . . here we are. You dropped in at just the right time. Saves me and Whitey considerable trouble, this does. Because we're ridin' south to see our good friend, Luke Lilavelt, and we wanted to take along some news that'll make him happy. Now we can. News that you're dead, Sutton . . . that . . ."

Dave Wall spoke, his tone hardly above a conversational level. "Look this way, Nick."

This whole play was a gamble and a desperate one. For Wall could read the drunken resolve in Nick, could see the utter certainty of it. Nick was going to kill. He was cocked and primed. Whether the idea had come before the whiskey was in him, or whether it was the whiskey that had set him off, there was no way of telling and it didn't matter. For the idea had him now, locked and deadly.

To have yelled at Nick might have startled him into pulling that trigger. To have shot him where he stood might have caused the same reaction. For a dying man's reflex had fired a gun before and even a man dead on his feet, once his gun was couched as Nick's was, could not have missed at the distance he stood from Bart Sutton. The only chance was to break through Nick's hard intentness without setting him off, and get him to swing that poised gun a little wide. After that . . .

Wall's quiet words cut through Nick Karnes's feral obsession. His round, small head swung and he saw Wall. It took a few long seconds for the full significance of Wall's presence to impinge on Nick's kill-drugged mind. In his black wicked eyes showed just a flicker of indecision and his gun wavered slightly.

Bart Sutton's right hand jerked and the contents of his half-lifted glass splashed in Nick's face. With the same move he was whirling away from the bar, going for his gun.

The small, thin tinkle of Sutton's dropped whiskey glass, splintering on the floor, came just ahead of the flat thunder of Nick Karnes's gun. Bart Sutton staggered, but held his feet. Nick, snake fast, was chopping down for a second try when Dave Wall let him have it, knowing he had to kill the venomous little rider, and shooting with that cold, dread purpose. For Bart Sutton couldn't have got there ahead of Nick's second try.

Dave Wall put his slug a little to the left of center in Nick Karnes's chest, heart high. The impact lifted Nick, drove him back a step, spun him slowly, and then dropped him in a loose, shrunken sprawl.

At his spot farther along the bar, Whitey Brewer got into belated action. Whitey had heard those first quiet words spoken by Dave Wall, but when Whitey jerked his head to locate them, Bart Sutton's solid bulk was between him and the saloon door and he was unable to locate Wall clearly. And then had come this crashing whirl of hard and deadly action that had put Nick sprawled and still on the floor.

But now the way to the door was open and Whitey saw Wall there. Whitey drew and fired all in one explosive move and the slug splintered through the wing door but inches away from where Wall's left hand still rested. It was Whitey's last conscious move, for now Bart Sutton had his gun clear and at its heavy roar Whitey fell back against the bar, slid down until he seemed to be sitting on the brass foot rail. Then he fell over on one side, his heels drummed twice, and then he was still.

The saloon, tied tight with motionless tension a

moment before, broke into confused action. Poker tables were deserted and men milled about, jostling and talking with the high hard tones that told of nerves that had been jangled and whipped raw by hovering danger and the violent release from it.

The ominous rumble and beat of gunfire had sent its sullen alarm well beyond the walls of The Rialto and men from other spots along the street came running to jam through the door. Among these were the four Window Sash hands who had ridden into town ahead of Wall and Tres Debley. Now, also, came Tres Debley and, catching the loom of Dave Wall's tall figure, bulled a way to his side. This brought Tres close enough in to see the sprawled figures of Nick Karnes and Whitey Brewer. Tres let out an explosive breath of relief.

"I expected to find either you or Bart Sutton down, Dave. I was afraid your talk had ended up in gunsmoke."

Dave Wall had been watching the crowd warily, particularly Olds and Challis and Muir and Caraway, not sure but that this thing might now move further. Harshly brief, he explained to Tres. "Karnes and Brewer had Sutton cornered and were set to get him. It worked out a better way. But Karnes got a slug into Sutton. Come on."

Wall used his elbows and the weight of his shoulders to drive through to Bart Sutton. The cattleman's jaw was set and pale lines bracketed his mouth. His left hand was pressed to his side.

"Where and how bad?" asked Wall.

"Not too bad, I guess," gritted Sutton. "Else I wouldn't still be on my feet. Felt like a horse kicked me . . . here." His hand pressed tighter against his side and an oozing crimson began to show about it. Dave Wall took him by the arm.

"This way. We'll have a look at it. Tres, keep an eye on the crowd, particularly on those four fine crewmates of ours."

There was a door opening off the far end of the bar. Dave steered Bart Sutton over to and through it. Here was what he had hoped, a back room with a bunk, a table, and a low-turned lamp. Dave turned up the lamp and said: "Sit down on that bunk."

He helped Sutton out of his calfskin vest and tan woolen shirt. The wound ran all across Sutton's side and was bleeding freely. Dave traced it carefully and then spoke with quick relief.

"You were lucky. Looks like the slug came in at a glancing angle, hit a rib, and skidded right along it before coming out. Might have cracked the rib and hurts like hell, I know. Stretch out and take it easy."

Sutton obeyed with a grunt of relief, and as Wall went back to the door of the room, the cattleman's eyes followed him, reflecting a puzzled wonderment.

Wall yelled at the bartender. "Some whiskey, some clean water, and fresh bar towels. Then send for a doctor!"

The bartender, white-faced and sweating, came hurrying. "Nary doctor in these parts," he gulped. "Sutton . . . he's hurt bad?"

"Not too bad. No doctor in this town, eh? Well, we'll do our best. Got some balsam oil?"

"No. But I think there might be some at the livery barn."

"Get it. Put that stuff on the table."

Bart Sutton took a pull at the whiskey bottle, and then lay in stoic silence while Dave Wall washed the wound and staunched the bleeding with wet compresses. The puzzlement in his glance deepened. "I can't figure you, Wall," he mumbled.

"Don't try," murmured Wall. "Sometimes I can't figure myself."

Tres Debley came in with the balsam oil, and Wall poured the wound full of the cooling, healing, aromatic stuff. He smiled grimly.

"Good for horses, good for humans. I've seen it heal far worse than this."

He folded clean bar towels across the wound and bound these firmly in place with strips Tres Debley tore from other towels. "That should do until we get you home. Think you can make the ride?"

The first shock was wearing off. Bart Sutton

sat up and reached for his shirt. "I'll make it," he said gruffly.

They helped him don his shirt and vest, but when Tres offered the whiskey bottle again the cattleman shook his head. "I'll make it," he said again.

Wall took a look at the barroom. The place was clearing. The four Window Sash hands had disappeared. The bodies of Karnes and Whitey Brewer had been carried off somewhere and where they had lain a man was busy with a mop and water bucket. The bartender came into the back room, honestly concerned.

"Good to see you on your feet, Bart. Those two . . . !" He shook his head. "They seemed to go crazy all of a sudden."

"Forget it, Sam," growled Sutton. "It's over now and no fault of yours." He turned and faced Dave Wall. "I say again that I can't figure you, Wall. It would have made things so simple for you and Lilavelt if you'd let them smoke me down. Instead, you stepped in just in time, downed Karnes, and wangled me a break against Brewer. Which left you minus two Window Sash hands while definitely saving my life. All of which leaves me wondering why and what for?"

"I got rid of Karnes and Brewer earlier today," said Wall. "Fired the pair of them. They were Lilavelt's men, not mine."

69

"That don't add up. You're a Lilavelt man yourself."

"I balk at murder," said Dave Wall briefly. "Let's get out of here."

Bart Sutton smiled twistedly. "I'm still fighting my head. But every man, I suppose, has some kind of a creed. I'm glad yours reads the way it does."

Wall said: "Get the horses, Tres. And while you're at it, look the street over." Wall was still remembering Olds, Challis, Muir, and Caraway. Out at the Crimson Hills headquarters they had not interfered in any way when he had taken the edge off Nick Karnes and Whitey Brewer, but there was no way of telling what they might be up to now.

Tres Debley, understanding thoroughly, nodded. He was soon back. "All set," he announced briefly. "And . . . all clear."

When they got Bart Sutton out to his horse and into the saddle, Sutton let out a deep sigh. "I don't know how I'm going to fight you, Wall. You take all my weapons away from me. Last night you did my daughter a decent turn. Tonight you saved my life and killed a Lilavelt man to do it. That leaves me dangling where you're concerned."

All Wall said was: "We're seeing you home, Tres and me."

"No need," rumbled the cattleman. "I can make it alone. I'm all right now."

"Maybe you are. Right now you got a stiff jolt of whiskey holding you up. It'll die out long before you get home. We're riding with you."

They went out of town at a walk, climbed the switchback trail up the lava rim, then swung away to the east. They rode in silence, each man locked in his own thoughts. They were halfway to Sweet Winds before Bart Sutton's shoulders began to sag a little. Dave and Tres moved up on either side of Sutton, just in case. But the grim old cattleman, though humped low and holding onto his saddle horn with both hands, definitely a sick man, was still riding without assistance when they pulled to a halt before the Square S ranch house.

The place was quiet and dark. They helped Sutton from his saddle and guided his now uncertain steps to the door. Dave Wall knocked and knocked again. Finally there was a stir in the house and a gleam of light. Then came Tracy Sutton's voice, sleepy but holding a growing note of alarm.

"Yes? Who is it?"

"This is Dave Wall, Miss Sutton. Your father's here. He's been hurt some."

There came a little wailing cry and the door was flung wide. Tracy Sutton was wrapped to the chin in a woolen robe. Her hair lay across her shoulders, loose yet shining in the light of the lamp she carried. Her face, flushed from inter-

71

rupted slumber, was now showing a deepening pallor and her eyes were deep, shadowed pools of terror as she glimpsed her father's sagging, weary-looking figure.

"Dad! Oh, Dad, what have they done to you? What . . . ?"

"I'm all right, child," broke in Sutton. "A little tuckered, that's all. Show these fellows where I sleep."

Chapter Four

Tracy Sutton led the way to a bedroom, added the glow of another lamp to the one she carried. The room was comfortable, well-furnished, the bed neatly made up. Bart Sutton flattened out on this, closed his eyes. The white-faced girl flayed Dave Wall with a glance.

"I wonder at your nerve, bringing him home, after . . . after . . . !"

"Steady, Trace . . . steady," rumbled Bart Sutton, his eyes still closed. "Don't jump at conclusions. Wasn't either of these who bounced a slug off my ribs. Somebody else did that, and they'd have made a complete job on me if Wall hadn't stepped in when he did. Child, I don't know why, but right now I'd like nothing better than a big cup of hot coffee. Run along and get it and I'll tell you all about this, after."

Tears brimmed and ran down her white cheeks as she bent over her father. She could see the ominous area that had stained his shirt now. "Oh, Dad . . . how bad is it? Dad . . . !"

Wall's voice ran gentle. "Not too bad, really. A few days in bed, that's all." He began pulling off Sutton's boots. "If you'll get that coffee for him, Tres and me will get him into bed."

"That's right," agreed Sutton. "Run along, child."

She left the room half hesitantly, as though reluctant to believe or to leave her father alone with Wall and Tres Debley. Working swiftly, they had Sutton between sheets before she got back, and after a survey of the wounded side, Wall straightened cheerfully.

"Bleeding entirely stopped," he announced, tucking the bandage back into place. "Be a little tender for a time, but if you don't rush matters, you'll be as fit as ever in a couple of weeks."

Sutton smiled up at him grimly. "Won't be able to keep that date to ride Window Sash range and look for blotted brands tomorrow, Wall. But I intend to go through with it before long. Luke Lilavelt won't rob me and get away with it. You can tell him I said so."

"Plain talk and necessary." Wall nodded. "I'll tell him."

Tracy Sutton came in with the coffee. Bart Sutton sat up and drank gratefully, nodding over the steaming cup. "Just what I needed. Takes right hold."

The girl had steadied. Some color was back in her face. Quietly she said: "Now, Dad . . . tell me."

Wall picked up his hat and moved to the door. "Debley and I will be getting along. Good luck."

Sutton said: "Take a good look at that man, Tracy. I don't know why, but tonight he saved my life. Wall . . . obliged."

The girl followed them to the door, saying nothing. And when night's outer dark had closed about him, Dave Wall still retained the picture of her as she stood there, slim and appealing in her shrouding robe, lamplight shining on the tumbled but fetching disarray of her hair.

The black chill of morning's very early hours lay over the world when Dave Wall and Tres Debley turned their horses in at the home corral. Tres said, as he headed for the bunkhouse: "I won't be quitting for a while, Dave. I'll be riding with you. I've got a strange feeling about things. Good night."

There were other saddles along the saddle pole and the blankets spread on top of them still smelled of warm horseflesh. This indicated that the other four Window Sash riders had come in from town not too long before. Dave laid a long glance on the dark and silent bunkhouse and on the equally dark and silent cook shack where Hippo Dell slept. In the light of the past night's violent happenings, he wondered what reactions would come from the men who slept there.

Well, it didn't particularly matter, he thought grimly. A hard and savage pattern that had held him prisoner for a long time was now beginning to break up. Circumstances unexpected and unplanned for had thrown a decision in his face and forced an answer. Anything could happen from now on. "Good night, Tres," he said.

He lay for some time on his bunk in the cabin, staring up at the black ceiling with wide, sleepless eyes. He was seeing and hearing many things again. That first stark, fixed picture when he stepped into The Rialto. His own intuitive reaction, the swift, harsh blasting of gunfire, dead men on the floor. The vast relief he had known when he saw that Bart Sutton's wound was not serious.

He was hearing again that little wailing cry of Tracy Sutton's, on realizing her father was hurt. And seeing again the terror in her wide eyes. Remembering the picture she had made with the lamplight shining on her hair and shoulders. Remembering also the savage, hating look she had thrown at him before she understood, and then her bewilderment just before he and Tres Debley left.

All these things he lay and thought about and with the thinking came the inevitable realization that here, in these Crimson Hills, he, Dave Wall, had come to a dead-end, so far as his usefulness to Luke Lilavelt was concerned. It wasn't any concern over the fact that in siding Bart Sutton he'd directly and indirectly put two of Lilavelt's riders dead on a saloon floor. He knew what Luke Lilavelt's reaction to that would be, but he didn't care. It was the sudden, but definite change within himself that made the big difference.

You couldn't, he thought, save a man's life and then set out to ruin him. You couldn't bring calamity and sorrow down on the head of a girl like Tracy Sutton. Tres Debley had put it right. There were some jobs a man could not tackle and still go on believing himself even a thin shadow of a man. This was that kind of a job. Right here, right now, Dave Wall knew that he was all through with Luke Lilavelt and the Window Sash.

What about the Connells? What about Judith and Jerry and the kids? Their future welfare and happiness were so completely tied in with his relationship with Luke Lilavelt, so dependent upon it. The day he cut loose from Lilavelt, that day he turned Lilavelt's malignancy loose upon the Connells. This thing he had endured so much to prevent, now had to be, and it was up to him to seek some other answer to protect Judith and Jerry and the kids. He had ridden the dark trails long enough—maybe too long ever to emerge fully into the light again. But it came to him that here at last, for better or worse, he was his own man again.

Strangely enough, now that this decision had been brought about, he felt an ease and relaxation he had not known for years. It flowed through him like a soothing current and he closed his eyes and slept. Later, roused slightly to a thin borderline between sleep and wakefulness, he thought, almost dream-like, that he heard the soft clop of hoofs, moving off into the night. The sound died out before he could come fully awake, so he drifted off again and slept soundly until the jangle of the breakfast gong awakened him.

Cold water on his face and neck brought him up to the full vigor of the day. His step carried a new spring to it as he crossed to the cook shack. The others were there ahead of him, but there was one missing. "Where's Muir?" he asked curtly.

There was no answer. Then Tres Debley said dryly: "I was wondering about that myself. He was in his bunk when I turned in last night, Dave."

Dave laid his glance on the others—Challis, Olds, and Caraway. "Well? You got any answers?"

Olds shrugged. "He came home with us and was in his blankets when we went to sleep. He was gone when we woke up this morning. His saddle's gone, too. That's all I know."

Dave looked at Challis and Caraway. "What do you think?"

Challis, a surly sort, grunted. "Olds told it all."

Dave took his seat, his eyes pinched and thoughtful. He recalled the faint sound of hoofs he'd heard, which had seemed almost dream-like at the time. His glance lifted to Hippo Dell's broad back, where Hippo stood busy over his stove.

"How about you, Dell? You got any idea of what could have sent Muir riding off so mysteriously?"

Hippo came around, ponderous yet light. His moon face told not a thing, his fat-bulwarked eyes even less. "I turned in early last night. Never even heard you fellers come home. But from what I've heard this morning, maybe Joe Muir figgered this outfit was too unhealthy to hang around." There was a moist, slurring inflection in Hippo's final statement.

"Meaning . . . what?" shot back Dave Wall. "What did you hear this morning, Hippo?"

"Why," said Hippo, "I heard that last night you sided Bart Sutton against Nick Karnes and Whitey Brewer, that you gunned Nick and watched Sutton do the same to Whitey. Only natural that Muir would wonder about that. I'm wondering myself."

"Wondering what, Hippo?" Wall's tone took on a slight crackle.

Hippo Dell seemed to square himself. "Wondering what the hell it means when the ramrod of an outfit guns down his own men to save the neck of . . ."

"Not my men," cut in Wall. "I fired Karnes and Brewer yesterday. I also issued orders that Square S and everything connected with it was to be left alone. Karnes and Brewer knew where I stood. Maybe you don't like that stand, Hippo?"

Hippo's eyes seemed to sink a little deeper

behind the rolls of fat. He shrugged, and turned back to his stove. "You're the boss," he said.

Wall recalled again what Tom Burke had said about Hippo Dell. Burke had mentioned Hippo, right after saying that he felt Luke Lilavelt had a spy at this headquarters. Maybe Hippo was that spy. Or maybe Joe Muir was it. Maybe that was where Muir had gone now, riding to tell Lilavelt about last night's ruckus, and of Wall's siding Bart Sutton and saving Sutton's life. This made sense, and Wall knew what he had to do.

He bent all his attention to his breakfast, finished as the others got up from the table. He looked up and said: "Just a minute there. I'm going to be away for a few days. Tres Debley is in charge. Any man who isn't willing to take Debley's orders can have his time. What about it?"

Olds said: "Suits me if it suits you, Wall."

This seemed to be the reaction of Challis and Caraway, so Wall let it lay that way.

Tres Debley followed Wall over to the corrals and watched him catch up a pair of fast horses. "Anything for my ears alone, Dave?"

"Yeah. I'm all through with Luke Lilavelt."

Tres hit his hands together, definitely pleased. "Why, now, that makes a pair of us. I'll ride with you, and to hell with this layout."

Wall shook his head. "No, Tres. You got to stick around. I'll be coming back, and you've got to keep the outfit in line until I do. That means, keeping them away from Square S. No telling what they might cook up if left to themselves. I've a feeling there's plenty more to Hippo Dell than just fat. I don't trust that man. And you see, Tres . . . while I'm all done with Lilavelt in one way, I'm just starting for him in another."

Tres Debley looked long into Dave Wall's eyes, then smiled faintly. They understood each other, these two. "Hurry back, man," drawled Tres. "I look to the future with interest. Good luck."

Dave Wall rode south and east from the Crimson Hills and he rode fast. This time his outfit was most meager, only what he could stuff into his saddlebags. The horse that followed at lead was a relay bronco, carrying nothing until, after several speedy miles, Dave pulled up and switched his saddle to the fresh animal. Traveling this way, using the horses alternately, he covered the long miles twice as fast as he had coming in.

The sun arched across the long, hot day. In the first blue dusk, Dave saw, off to his left, the distant cluster of winking lights that marked the town of Cottonwood. But they held no lure for him, and they drifted behind and were lost in the night. Sixteen hours after leaving the Crimson Hills, Dave shuffled his weary horses up to a little ranch house standing in a meadow in a bend of Magpie Creek.

The place was dark, for it lacked but an hour of midnight. Dave stepped down and stood for a moment, waiting for the feel of the earth to come up through his stiffened legs. He was thoroughly saddle beat, gaunt with fatigue. He watered his horses at the creek, then unsaddled and turned them into a corral where feed racks loomed spectrally in the light of a late-rising, lop-sided moon. He hung his gear on the corral fence and went over to the house. His knocking brought movement, the murmur of voices, and then a light. A wiry, brown, thin-faced young fellow with electric blue eyes, clad in jeans and undershirt opened the door. He held a lamp in his left hand, but carried his right slightly behind him.

Dave Wall grinned crookedly. "You won't need the gun, Jerry. It's only me."

"Dave!" exclaimed Jerry Connell. "Man . . . I'm glad to see you. Come in . . . come in! Judy, it's that big rough, tough brother of yours!"

There was an excited feminine murmur, a hurrying rush, and then Dave was in the arms of his only sister, Mrs. Jerry Connell. He gave her a mighty hug, then held her off at arm's length and looked at her fondly.

"A little more the matron, but still the prettiest girl this side of the desert."

"Oh . . . oh!" exclaimed Judith Connell. "It used to be in all of the state. Dave! Don't tell me that you, the confirmed lone wolf, have at last met . . . ?"

"Same old Judy," cut in Wall, grinning wearily. "Always jumping at conclusions. Suppose you do a little jumping around the kitchen instead? I saw food last at six this morning."

Judith lingered for a moment, staring up at him with anxious eyes. "It's not like you to come in at this time of night on a visit, Dave . . . not without cause. Is there . . . trouble?"

"Being half starved is reason enough, isn't it?" he teased.

"Well, maybe," she admitted reluctantly. She wasn't entirely satisfied, but she gave him another hug, then headed off to the kitchen.

Jerry Connell, studying Wall intently, said slowly: "Judy is pretty keen about such things. What is it, Dave?"

Wall turned a sober face, kept his voice low. "I guess we're going to have to face the big showdown, fellah. Sorry, but my hand is forced. I'm through with Lilavelt."

Jerry tipped a slow nod. "I'm glad," he said simply. "I really am, Dave. It will be a hell of a relief. I've been living with this thing so long now, seeing myself as only half a man with you making all the sacrifices. I want you to believe me when I say I was going to ask for the show-down the next time we got together. I'm in good shape now. Had a fine year. I don't owe a cent and I've got a fair little bank balance, enough to take care of Judy and the kids for quite a time. Yeah, this is it, Dave . . . and I tell you I'm glad."

"It's going to be mighty tough on Judy," reminded Wall.

"I know," agreed Jerry. "But she's the pure quill, with plenty of what it takes. I think she's half suspected something for some time now, for she's been after me and after me as to why you've stayed on with Lilavelt, and it's been pretty hard trying to figure out reasons. What happened, anyhow?"

Dave Wall shrugged. "He put me up against a job I just couldn't stomach. Call it that, or call it that the bottle was suddenly full and running over. All of a sudden I just found myself at the end of the trail. I don't want you to think I'm running out on you and Judy and the kids, Jerry. You know I'd never do that. But this thing . . ." He shrugged again.

"Run out be damned." Jerry Connell gripped Wall's arm tightly. "Show me another man who would have done for anyone what you've done for Judy and me. I tell you this had to come . . . and I'm glad."

"You make it easier for me, Jerry." Wall smiled. "How are the kids?"

"Great. The twins are a pair of young hellions. And little Judy . . . she's her mother all over again. Dave, if I can shake out from under that one fool mistake, I'll be the happiest man alive."

"You will, fellah. Lilavelt has bought himself the fight of his life." A thread of harshness crept into Wall's voice and dark bleakness shadowed his face. "I made him a couple of promises. I'll keep them." Then his mood lightened. "I smell coffee."

They sat across the kitchen from him while he ate, Jerry intent with sober thoughts, Judith with her chin cupped in her hands, her fair hair loose across her robe-clad shoulders, her eyes resting on him with probing intentness.

"You've grown older, Brother mine. You've lost weight. You're lean as a whip. It's been a long time between visits. What have you been doing? Tell us about yourself."

"Nothing to tell, Judy. I ride here. I ride there. Time passes and, well . . . that's about all."

"No it isn't," she differed shrewdly. "There's a look about the pair of you. Come on . . . tell Sister."

Wall met Jerry's glance. "I think," he said slowly, "that the telling rightly belongs to Jerry."

"That's right," Jerry said, clearing his throat. "And when I'm done, I hope you still love me."

Judith swung her head, looked at her husband. Her gray eyes grew big and dark, but steady. "As long as it isn't another woman, Jerry . . . nothing else matters. I've known for a long time that you had something on your mind and I've waited, feeling that in your own good time you'd tell me. Go ahead."

Jerry captured one of her hands. "It could never be another woman," he said simply. "This, my dear, is the story of a fool."

And then he told it, simply and bluntly. It was the story of reckless, heedless youth, of too much trust in a man not worthy of it, and of an extra glass or two of liquor that tipped recklessness over to foolhardiness.

"It was in New Mexico," Jerry said. "I was a kid of eighteen, riding for Sam Larkin's Broken Arrow. We'd been three months without sight of a town. We were pretty woolly when we hit Round Mountain. There was a man in the crew named Big George Yearly. To a rattle-weeded kid he was quite a man. I thought he was the greatest guy in the world. Well, in Round Mountain I drank more than was good for me and along with some of the others ended up in a gambling layout, bucking the tiger. We were ripe for a shearing and we got it. Three months' wages were gone in jig time. We went outside and got to talking it over. Big George Yearly claimed the table was crooked. It might have been, at that. Anyhow, that was when the damn' foolishness really started."

Jerry paused, poured himself a cup of coffee, nursed it between both hands.

"Big George suggested that we get our money back. We were to wait until the crowd had thinned out and the joint about to close for the night. Then we'd barge in and get our money back. At the time it seemed like a right fine idea. Big George made it sound all right. They had, so he put it, really stolen our money by using a crooked table, so it was only fair for us to go get it back at gunpoint. As I say, it seemed like a right fine idea, about then."

Judith Connell stirred slightly. Looking at her, Dave Wall saw that her face was paling.

Jerry went on doggedly. "We drew straws to see who would stay with the horses. I got that job. Big George and the others went in after the money. They didn't get it. It wasn't that simple or easy. There was shooting. Three men besides Big George went into the joint. Only Big George came out alive. He came in a hurry, running for his horse. The shooting had stirred up the town. The night marshal showed. He yelled at Big George to stop. Big George didn't. The night marshal threw a shot, but missed. Big George threw one back and the marshal went down."

Jerry took a deep drag of coffee, his eyes bleak with old memories.

"Big George hit leather and rode for it. He didn't wait for me or pay me any attention at all. He just hit leather and rode. I never saw him again. I forked my horse and lit out, too. I kept going, clear out of New Mexico. For the next couple of years all I did was ride and ride. I'd stop in some place only long enough to earn a little stake and then I'd cut loose and hit the trail again. Finally I ended up here . . . and met you, Judith."

The next moment Dave Wall was very proud of this sister of his. Color had come back into her cheeks, a faint smile touched her lips, and her eyes were soft and fond as she leaned over and took her husband's hand.

"I've only one little bit of censure for you, my dear. That you didn't tell Dave all this before."

"I did tell him," said Jerry. "I told him all about it before asking his permission to marry you."

"Why, then," said Judith Connell softly, "you're still the very perfect husband. And you were afraid, all this time, to tell me? Foolish man. It doesn't amount to a thing. You did nothing, actually. You did no shooting. You hurt no one. We'll just forget it all."

"It isn't going to be that easy, my dear," Jerry told her soberly. "You've wondered and wondered why Dave has worked for Luke Lilavelt? Well, somehow, some way, Lilavelt heard of that New Mexico trouble and my part in it. And he's used that knowledge as a club over Dave's head ever since, driving Dave to do jobs for him he could never have hired done, no matter how much money he paid."

Judith looked at Dave and began to cry. "Dave.

For me . . . for us . . . you've given years . . . darkened your name . . . Oh, I've heard what people have said about you . . . how you were Luke Lilavelt's right-hand man when the job was so rough and savage nobody else. . . . Oh, Dave . . . you've given so much. . . ."

"There, there," comforted Wall quickly. "We talked it over, Jerry and I did, after Lilavelt showed his cards. The twins were little guys then, just six months old, and Jerry was just getting this ranch going pretty well. We considered the future and figured the more evidence of good faith and sound citizenship we could pile up on Jerry's part, the better break and chance for leniency he'd get in a court of law when we finally opened the books. And, of course, the more chance for a good future for you and the kids. We went at it with our eyes open. We knew what we were doing. So don't you weep over me, old girl. I'm doing all right. And so is Jerry. For now we're going to have a little showdown with Mister Luke Lilavelt. Tomorrow, Jerry and I head for Basin, to have a talk with Judge Masterson. And we're going to lay all the cards on the table."

Judith made no effort to stop the tears. She went from one to the other of them, hugging them and murmuring something about the two finest men in the world.

It was far after midnight when they ceased talking and making plans. Judith went and made up a spare bunk for Dave, and then led him into the small corner room where the children slept. She held a shaded lamp while Dave looked. His eyes softened and he touched small, dreamless heads with a gentle finger.

"Put all three of 'em in my hip pocket at once, almost," he murmured. "Yet they're the biggest things in the world. I ain't got one thin regret, Judy."

He thought of this again before he fell asleep. Not a single regret for what the past had cost him, so long as it helped those little ones and Judith and Jerry. The thought held him still and musing. And then he thought of Luke Lilavelt, the man who held a club over this family, who would see it broken up and wickedly hurt just to advance his own greedy, tricky ends.

Dave Wall grew rigid under his blankets, caught up with a cold and bitter hate. Luke Lilavelt had made him into something that other men feared and avoided, made him a dark legend across the better part of the state. Well, Lilavelt had created something that had now turned on him, unleashed a force that, if he lived, vowed Wall, would grind Luke Lilavelt down and smash him as he had smashed others.

It was a hard thought to carry into sleep, but when sleep came all that went away and Wall relaxed fully, as though comforted by the subconscious knowledge that the trail had taken a right-angled turn and that a new and better future was beckoning.

He was awakened by Judith shaking his shoulder. Cool dawn lay outside. Judith's voice was shaky.

"Sheriff Cole Ashabaugh is at the door, Dave. He . . . he's come for Jerry. I . . . I want you there when Jerry faces him."

Wall dressed swiftly, his thoughts winging. This could mean only one thing. Luke Lilavelt had got word of that affair in Crater City, that shoot-out that had put Nick Karnes and Whitey Brewer dead on a saloon floor, and of his part in the picture. There was only one way Lilavelt could have got the news this quickly, and that was through Joe Muir, the saddle hand who had sneaked away from the Crimson Hills headquarters in the dark of night. And now Lilavelt had retaliated, struck swiftly, doing what he had threatened all along, should Wall ever turn against him and his interests. He had opened the door of Jerry Connell's past.

Wall set his gun belt about his lean middle with hard jerks. *All right, Mister Luke Lilavelt,* he thought grimly. *You've made good your promise. Now I'll make good on mine. War is what you've asked for, war is what you get. No holds barred, no quarter asked, no quarter given. War . . . to the last bitter, hating breath.*

Sheriff Cole Ashabaugh was grizzled and lank,

91

with harsh eyes, bleak and blue. Wall said: "Hello, Cole. What's on your mind?"

Looking at Wall, the cold glint sharpened in Ashabaugh's eyes, reflecting no friendliness at all. "Some things," said the sheriff, "I've never been able to understand at all."

Wall knew what he meant. Here it was again, the same old barrier of distrust and dislike that had risen to meet him in men he had once called friends. All since he had worked for Luke Lilavelt.

"Cole," he said curtly, "do you say howdy to Lilavelt when you meet him on the street?"

It was a telling shot and a faint tide of red stained Cole Ashabaugh's leathery cheeks. Luke Lilavelt was a political power in the county and those who held public office played their cards accordingly. The sheriff turned and looked past Wall at Jerry Connell.

"You know why I'm here, Connell. I got a warrant for your arrest, drawn and sworn to in Judge Masterson's office, charging you with complicity in attempted armed robbery and in the murder of Night Marshal Charles Ogden, in the town of Round Mountain, New Mexico. You'll come along quiet?"

"Of course, Sheriff," said Jerry.

Ashabaugh's glance went to Judith, standing at her husband's side, very pale of face and wide of eye. He touched his hat and slightly awkwardly said: "I ain't enjoying this a bit, Missus Connell."

Dave Wall headed out to the corrals, catching up and saddling horses for Jerry and himself. As he walked back to the ranch house, leading the animals, Cole Ashabaugh moved out to meet him.

"I came out here after Jerry Connell," said the sheriff pointedly. "There's no call for you to mix in, Wall."

"So?" retorted Wall. "Well, I'm mixing, Cole. I'm mixing plenty in a lot of things from here on out. Things are a lot different than they were ten days ago. I'm a free man again. You wouldn't know what I mean by that, but it's a fact. And so I'm looking forward to telling off a lot of proud damned hypocrites."

Again that faint flush touched Ashabaugh's face. He was twisting up a cigarette. "Damned broad statement, Wall. Think you're in the position to make it?"

A faintly crooked, completely mirthless smile quirked Wall's lips. "Cole, you'd be surprised."

Jerry Connell kissed his wife, went straight to his horse, and stepped into the saddle. Judith looked at him, twisting her hands, then whirled to Wall.

"Dave. You'll see . . . you'll take care . . . ?"

Her voice husked and choked up. Dave Wall put an arm around her, his voice very gentle. "Old girl, have I ever let you down? Don't worry. A lot of whelps are going to be kicked back into their kennels. Come on . . . chin up."

She hugged and kissed him, and then managed a strained, white little smile and a wave as they rode off. Wall, swinging in beside the sheriff, drawled: "You must feel like a hell of a big man, Cole, at a time like this. Yeah, you must feel big and noble and proud . . . for when you slapped this arrest on Jerry, you were doing some dirty work for Luke Lilavelt."

Ashabaugh swung a savage head. "Don't try and rawhide me, Wall. I'm merely carrying out the duty of my office, and you know it. I told your sister I wasn't enjoying it, didn't I?"

Wall's slightly mocking grin worked again. "Ah. That good old shield of duty. Sure handy to hide behind, Cole. But you know who swore out that warrant, don't you? So do I. That esteemed citizen, Mister Luke Lilavelt. So, when you serve it, you're working for him. Oh, don't run a fever, Cole. I know how it is. I know exactly how it is."

Cole Ashabaugh ground his teeth but did not answer. He stared straight ahead and Dave Wall let things ride that way. He was fully aware of the truth of the sheriff's statement. In arresting Jerry Connell, Cole Ashabaugh was merely fulfilling a sworn duty; he had no other choice. Secretly Wall had always liked Ashabaugh. As sheriffs went, he was a good one. But in his new-found sense of freedom, Dave wouldn't have been wholly human if he hadn't found some satisfaction in needling a man who had taken to looking askance at him ever since he'd been riding for Lilavelt. Actually he held nothing against Ashabaugh for that, because the sheriff, like a lot of others, didn't understand. But he got a sort of morbid pleasure in watching Ashabaugh squirm.

They rode into Basin at midmorning and pulled up in front of Judge Masterson's office. As they swung down, Wall said: "You might as well wait for me, Cole, because I'm going to see Jerry through this, all the way, every step of the way. I won't be long."

Before the sheriff could answer, Wall was striding swiftly along the street, an unconscious, forward-leaning eagerness in his manner. He went as far as Luke Lilavelt's office, tried the door, and found it locked. He cupped his hands about his face and peered in at the window. The office was definitely empty, so he turned away and came back to the sheriff and his prisoner.

Ashabaugh looked at him with a measuring intentness. "Nobody home, I gather. What would you have done if there had been?"

"Why," answered Dave with sudden grimness, "I'd have slapped around one of the world's lowest whelps. Yeah, I'd have slapped the raw hell out of him. I'd have tried to make him go for a gun, and when he did, I'd have shot him to rags."

"That," said Ashabaugh, "sounds like you're riding along a pretty dangerous trail, Wall. I don't need to tell you, do I, that I won't stand for it?"

Wall showed him a small and wicked smile. He filled a deep chest and stretched a long and sinewy pair of arms. "Cole, until it's over with, you won't have a damned thing to say about it. Yeah, you're right. A dangerous trail, and I'm sure riding it."

Chapter Five

Judge James Masterson had a fine, stern face under a crown of snow-white hair. He was a man almost fanatically dedicated to the integrity of the law, to its exact science and letter and protocol. But he was a just man and, under his cloak of sternness, an intensely human one. His attitude toward Jerry Connell was grave but not unfriendly, but toward Dave Wall he was frigidly cool.

"I wish to talk to Mister Connell alone," he said. "Sheriff, you will leave us so, and take Mister Wall with you."

Dave said: "A moment, Judge. Understand, I'm not trying to tell you your business. But you're a fair man, and to be fair in this you'll have to hear all the story. And I'd like Cole Ashabaugh to hear it, too. I think you'll agree to the justice of what I ask, once you've heard what Jerry and I have to say."

Judge Masterson leaned his elbows on his desk and steepled his fingertips, while his glance searched Dave Wall's face. "I would hardly take it kindly, Mister Wall, if you are playing with the idea that you can in any way influence my judicial duty."

Now it was Jerry Connell who spoke up.

"Judge, Dave doesn't mean it that way at all. All he and I want is for you to know the truth. After we've given you that, you can take over from there and whatever you say and do will be more than all right with both of us."

The judge swung his eyes to Jerry. "Mister Connell, I presume Sheriff Ashabaugh has given you the gist of the warrant he holds. The warrant speaks of armed robbery . . . murder. Those are very serious charges, Mister Connell . . . very serious. A man accused of them is in no position to bargain, I can assure you of that. I would say that your smartest move would be to find a good attorney to represent you, stand on all your legal prerogatives and rights. Anything you say in front of Sheriff Ashabaugh could conceivably be used against you."

"I'm not trying to hedge or dodge in any way, Judge," said Jerry soberly. "I'm trying to clear up my life for the sake of my wife and family. If the truth won't clear it up, then nothing will. If a man can't ride on the truth and what it will bring him, then nothing is worth a damn, I guess."

The judge considered for some time in silence. Then he said dryly: "You have a certain per-suasiveness about you, Mister Connell. This is . . . er . . . somewhat irregular, but . . ." He leaned back in his chair, folded his hands in his lap. "Go ahead, Mister Connell. I'm listening."

Jerry went through with his story, just as he

had given it to Judith the night before. Judge Masterson listened without comment, his eyes never leaving Jerry's face. Not until Jerry finished did he speak.

"It would have helped your case a great deal if you'd have come to me long ago with these facts, Mister Connell. Why didn't you?"

"Maybe I can answer that, Judge," said Dave Wall. "It's pretty hard to turn your back on the future when you're young, when you've met and fallen in love with the only girl. And you can believe this or not, sir. But just last night Jerry and I decided to come to you and put all our cards on the table. Given another few hours and Sheriff Ashabaugh wouldn't have had to come after Jerry."

The judge studied Wall again. "Mister Connell is your brother-in-law, Mister Wall. You've been familiar with this ancient trouble of his for some time?"

"Jerry," said Wall quietly, "told me the whole story when he came to me asking permission to marry my sister."

"And you offered no objections, Mister Wall?"

"As I saw it, Judge, it took a pretty damned good man to act as squarely as Jerry did. He could have said nothing of his past trouble, gambling that it would never catch up with him. But he thought too much of my sister to do that. He put the cards on the table and they were good enough for me. And if every man was eternally damned for some fool, reckless mistake he'd made in his life, there'd be few of us who'd ever reach heaven."

It could have been a gleam of reflected sunlight pouring in at the office window, or it might have been the faintest suggestion of a twinkle, far back in Judge Masterson's eyes. He cleared his throat and dryly said: "Sage observation, Mister Wall. Which brings us to consideration of how this case will be handled."

"But there's more to tell, sir," said Jerry swiftly. "And this concerns Dave. Maybe, like others, you've wondered why a man like Dave Wall could stomach working for Luke Lilavelt?"

The judge was swiftly stern again. "We're not here to discuss Mister Lilavelt."

"We've got to," asserted Jerry doggedly, "if we're to get the whole picture, sir. Just how Luke Lilavelt got hold of that trouble of mine, I don't know. But he did. It was some time after Judith and I were married. I had my ranch going in pretty good shape and there were a couple of youngsters in the family by that time. Somehow Lilavelt heard of that Round Mountain affair. He cornered Dave, told him what he knew, and threatened to expose me unless Dave went to work for him and handled all sorts of mean jobs in Window Sash interests."

Jerry paused, running a lean hand through his

hair. Judge Masterson flashed a quick and startled look at Dave Wall, then turned his attention to Jerry once more, leaning forward in his chair, deeply interested.

"I felt like a damned coyote," went on Jerry, "letting Dave make a sacrifice like that, for I knew what it would mean to his good name. I was ready right then to come to you with the story. But Dave said no. He said this was something that had to be done to protect Judith and the children. He said it wasn't the right time to open the books, that what we had to do was get the ranch in better shape, get some money ahead, and show plenty of evidence of good intention toward being a decent citizen on my part. So that's the way it was, sir."

Both Judge Masterson and Sheriff Cole Ashabaugh were now staring at Dave Wall, and Ashabaugh in particular seemed increasingly ill at ease. The judge steepled his fingers again and fixed his glance on them, frowning. Once or twice he nodded, as though over sober inner thoughts. Finally he began to speak, with troubled slowness.

"I am being irregular in this, very irregular, but there seems to be no other solution. I admit I've wondered, many times over Luke Lilavelt's part in this. Several years ago it was when he first came to me, bringing a sealed envelope, asking that I keep it in my safe. His instructions were that the contents of the envelope remain unknown unless he came to claim it and open it in my presence, or in event of his sudden and violent death. In which case I was to open the envelope and act upon what the contents disclosed. Last evening Lilavelt did come to this office, asked for the envelope, and opened it. In it was this old Reward poster, or dodger as Sheriff Ashabaugh refers to it. On the basis of it, Lilavelt swore out the warrant of arrest."

Judge Masterson paused, glanced at Dave Wall. "You have said, Mister Wall, that you and Mister Connell had decided to come to me with the story, even if Sheriff Ashabaugh had not moved into the picture with the warrant of arrest. That suggests that you had broken with Lilavelt."

Wall nodded. "I had, Judge."

"May I ask why?"

Dave Wall was quiet for a moment, brooding. Then he shrugged. "Say that I'd gone just as far as I could. That I'd come to the point where I had to revolt. Word that I had was carried to Lilavelt, so he made good his threat to strike at Jerry. So, here we are."

The judge got a well-loved pipe from a desk drawer, loaded, and lit it, and puffed reflectively. "I am," he said slowly, "a great believer in the integrity of the law. I also hold firmly to the principle that violaters of the law be punished in proportion to the severity of the crime. However,

I am always willing to give full and fair consideration to any and all mitigating circumstances, and to consider the character of the defendant, both before and after. I also agree to a considerable extent with Mister Wall's theory that no man should be everlastingly damned for a single mistake, unless it be of the sort that is completely unforgivable. Your mistake, Mister Connell, was not of that sort. So here is what I shall do."

Judge Masterson leaned forward and his words and manner became crisp.

"There is only one way to handle this matter . . . one sound way. That is by due process of law. Let us say that our personal sentiments might be to tear up the warrant and forget the whole matter. But this would not dispose of the trouble permanently . . . you would always have the charge hanging over you. The only way to clear your name and guarantee your future and the happiness of your family, Mister Connell, is through the law and its processes. So I must and will get in contact with the authorities in New Mexico. It is quite possible, though I would not draw too much comfort from the thought, that they are no longer overly concerned with the affair. After all, it did happen some time ago, witnesses may have scattered and died, and the authorities there might feel that they could not, in any case, win a conviction. Such things have happened before. But we must find out about that. For the present, I have no other recourse than to remand you to the custody of Sheriff Ashabaugh. We will hope that the period of incarceration will not be too lengthy and you have my word that I will push for a speedy solution of the affair. And . . ."—here Judge Masterson's innate kindliness shone through— "I will also go to the greatest length to see that your interests are presented in the most favorable light."

Jerry Connell drew a deep breath and blurted boyishly: "Judge, you're one damned white man. Your judgment is good enough for me."

The judge's stern face lit up with a particularly warm and human smile. "You have a fine and lovely wife and a thriving young family, Mister Connell. We must all do our best by them."

Then Judge Masterson did another surprising thing. He got to his feet, moved around the desk to face Dave Wall, and held out his hand. "Will you do me the honor, Mister Wall?"

"It is my pleasure, sir," said Dave as their hands met.

They left the judge's office and now Jerry turned to Dave. "There'll have to be a good man out at the ranch, Dave. Somebody to keep the work caught up and keep an eye on things. I don't want Judy and the kids left out there alone. That damned Luke Lilavelt might try 'most anything if this scheme of his begins to backfire."

"You leave that to me," answered Dave. "And Judy will be in to see you regularly. There'll be no objection to that, will there, Sheriff?"

"You know damned well there won't," growled Cole Ashabaugh. "I want you to wait right here for me, Wall. All right, Jerry."

So Jerry Connell went off to jail and Dave Wall stood and looked the street over, while building a thoughtful cigarette. This thing was in the open now. All in all, thinking about it, Dave was satisfied with the way things were working out. Judge Masterson had been tolerant and fair. It was going to be a little rough on Jerry, cooling his heels behind bars. And it would be even rougher on Judy, for Dave well knew how proud she was. However, life was that way. No trail was ever completely smooth, and if the matter came out all right, the future for Judy and Jerry would be bright. Judge Masterson was completely right about the need of clearing Jerry's name, once and for all, by due process of the law.

Dave had smoked his cigarette down and tossed the butt into the street's warm dust when Cole Ashabaugh came stamping up. For a moment he stood at Dave Wall's side, saying nothing. Then he cleared his throat harshly.

"I guess I got an apology to make to you, Dave . . . so I'm making it. I had you all wrong as to why you worked for Lilavelt and let him push you around like you did."

Dave grinned and slapped him on the shoulder. "Forget it, Cole. You're not alone. A lot of people have wondered. Most of them have been fair enough, all things considered. A few have jumped at the chance to rub it in. Those I intend to educate at the first opportunity. I'm serving notice to that effect, right now. I hope you're not going to argue the point with me."

Cole Ashabaugh scraped a boot along the board sidewalk. "Within limits," he said gruffly, "I'll even wish you luck. But don't go hog wild, man. I don't want to have to come after you. Now, something else. About that good man to take over out at Connell's ranch. How would my brother Holt do? He just finished topping off a bunch of young saddle stuff for Henry Laramore last week and hasn't a thing on his mind right now but his hat."

"Couldn't pick a better man," agreed Dave. "If he'll do it."

"He'll do it," vowed Ashabaugh, "and be glad of the chance. He'll be on his way out to the ranch before sundown. Now, I'll buy a drink . . . if you'll do me the honor."

Their eyes met and they swapped hard grins. They understood each other completely. They tramped along to Mize Callan's Empire House, turned in to the cool, half gloom of the place. Among others, Oren White was there, thick-set, florid of face. White ran a small spread south of town, but was a man who was never going any place, because he gambled and drank up what profits his ranch brought in as fast as they accrued.

Once Oren White had laid ardent suit for Judith Wall's hand, before Jerry Connell came along to claim it completely. Judith had never cared for the man, though her nature would not let her be anything but pleasant toward him. Dave Wall had never liked White, either, but had not interfered in any way, confident that his sister's innate fineness and good judgment would not be overly impressed by White. This was how it had turned out and White, arrogant and intolerant and ever the poor loser, had turned sly venom on the Connells and particularly on Dave Wall, plainly showing that he felt that Dave had influenced Judith against him.

Dave's going to work for Luke Lilavelt, with the subsequent dark reputation this inevitably built, had furnished White with plenty of material to work on. In a number of different ways he had worked to turn public opinion against Dave, missing no opportunity to drive the knife ever deeper and to twist it more savagely.

The man was smooth and clever at this sort of thing. With a word, a look, a suspended motion, or turn of a shoulder, he managed to convey much. He was at the bar now, rolling one-flop poker dice for the drinks, with Mize Callan, Buck

Sorenson, and Pat Shea. As Dave Wall and Cole Ashabaugh faced the bar a little farther along, White said, *sotto voce*: "I heard a man saying something once about the dignity of the law. He must have been joking."

Dave Wall came around, his eyes going dark. That was Oren White for you, making a remark that could be interpreted two ways, and wanting it so. Though apparently directed at Cole Ashabaugh, the inferred slur was against the man Ashabaugh was drinking with, Dave Wall.

Before Dave could say a word, it was Ashabaugh who shot it back at Oren White, shot it fast and harsh. "White, you save my self-respect. I thought I'd been the biggest damn' fool in the state. I was wrong. I was only the second biggest. You win first prize in a walk-away. And besides me, there's a flock of lesser fools, some of them present. Mize . . . a little service!"

Mize Callan, always a tough man, put out bottle and glasses, growling: "Cole, when you've been eating raw meat, best wait until the effect wears off before you land in here all spraddled out. Just because you wear a badge gives you no license to come into my place and label me a fool. Cut it fine."

"Mize," said the sheriff, "I'm going to tell you a story. Then I'll let you be the judge."

"No, Cole," cut in Dave Wall swiftly. "We just came in here for a drink, not to beat any drums.

As for White, his mouth has always been bigger than his brain. He just naturally can't help drooling."

Raw color turned Oren White's naturally florid face a brick red. He slammed down the dice box, pushed past Buck Sorenson and Pat Shea.

"Wall, you may be a tough cookie with that gun on, but . . ."

Dave made two swift jerks with his hands and his belt and holstered gun fell to the floor.

"Not on now, White. You full of ambition?"

Mize Callan slapped a hard palm on the bar top. "Wall, I warned you once before not to start. . . ."

Now it was Cole Ashabaugh who cut in, his tone dryly cold. "Mize, you keep damn' well out of this. I mean . . . out! Some things can only be settled one way. This is one of them. Take your gun off, White . . . or make your little bow and back down."

This was the way it could be with Cole Ashabaugh when he thought the occasion warranted it. A streak of toughness had jumped out of him that gave them all pause. His blue eyes burned with a cold flame.

Mize Callan shrugged and put both hands on the bar. Buck Sorenson and Pat Shea stepped well back, Sorenson saying mildly: "I never begrudge room to them who need it to ruff their feathers in. I'm willing to watch. I might even enjoy it."

Cole Ashabaugh's voice was whip sharp. "I'm

waiting, White. Shuck that gun and show the color of your marbles. You've been making a certain kind of talk much too big and for much too long. So now you flap your wings, or you crawl."

Oren White cursed, shucked belt and gun. And then he went straight in at Dave Wall, head pulled deep between his meaty shoulders and with both fists swinging.

Dave ducked one flailing punch, took another on the point of a hunched shoulder, and got home a solid wallop of his own under Oren White's heart. But it was not enough to stop White's charge, so now they came together heavily and lurched into the bar. There was not much to choose between the two of them where weight was concerned, but Dave was a little the taller, raw-boned where White was thick and burly.

White had a shoulder against Dave's chest and with thick legs spread and braced, held Dave against the bar, while he slammed both fists against Dave's board-hard midriff. The man could hit. The punches hurt, sending Dave's breath rocketing up into his throat.

Dave pushed his right hand up, inside, got the heel of it under White's chin, and, even as White hit him twice more in the body, put everything he had into a savage lift. The effort snapped White's head back, sent him whirling aside, and Dave got clear of the bar, shifting swiftly to catch

White coming back in and nailing him with a driving smash to the face. The blow brought blood and shook up White, stopping his rush completely. He gave back a couple of steps, scrubbed a hand across his bloody mouth.

Dave Wall was glad of this short respite. Those four solid body wallops White had landed had not done Dave a bit of good and he fought hungrily for air. One thing he knew. He had to keep away from this man and not let him get in on the same target again, at least not until the first effects began to wear off. That was how it was with body punishment—it stayed with you. A blow to the head might stun and daze momentarily, but could soon be shaken off. Not so with body wallops. They dragged you down, took it out of you.

Oren White seemed to understand what was going on in Dave Wall's mind, for now he gathered himself and came in once more with that low, heavy rush. Dave side-stepped and belted him across the temple as he went by. It was the hardest blow Dave had so far got across and it knocked White floundering into a poker table that skidded off at a wild angle and let White down with a crash. He rolled over, got to his hands and knees, and stayed there for a short moment, shaking his head. Then he came up again, crouched and a little more wary.

Now Dave began moving in. He speared a long,

battering left to White's crimsoned mouth, feinted with his right, then put two more of those lashing lefts to White's sore lips. These seemed to madden White, for he bawled a hoarse curse and came in with another headlong, pawing rush. This time Dave did not try and side-step. Instead, he set himself, dropped his knees together, and lifted his right fist into White's body, just under the heart. It was a duplicate of the first punch Dave had landed in the fight, but much harder, carrying everything he had behind it. It hurt Oren White wickedly.

Breath came out of him in an explosive gasp, almost a groan, and the punch seemed to hang him on his toes, while his pawing hands flailed, wild and useless. Then he came down on one knee, both hands flat on the floor for support. His head rocked from side to side like that of a wounded bear, and blood dribbled down from his sagging, battered lips. His eyes glared up in bitter hate and the pulse of fury throbbed in his throat and temples.

He reached a pawing hand, got hold of a round-backed chair, used it as a support to get to his feet again. Then he steadied himself, swung the chair high, and threw it at Wall. Dave couldn't avoid the thing, so took the impact on outthrust and fending arms and, as the chair glanced aside, knew a gust of gray and blinding rage. Up to this point the fight had been reasonably straight up and down, fists against fists. But if this was the way White wanted it, Dave swarmed at his man, beating down White's thick arms, clubbing him to the face and body. He got an arm around White's neck, got a hip under him, and threw him, hard. From the floor White kicked Dave's feet from under him and now they were both down, locked and rolling. Dave got a knee in the ribs and an elbow in the mouth and tasted the swift salt of his own blood. He got a blind fist in the center of the forehead and things grew dull and sluggish in him. He managed to pull clear and lurch to his feet again, and it felt as though some enormous weight were on his shoulders.

White got up even more slowly. His mouth was wide open and every reach he made for air was a raw and sobbing gasp. Wall went for him with short, spread-legged steps. His fists seemed cased in invisible weights, for it took a distinct effort to raise each one and push it at White. But they traveled and they hit, and White's head rolled weakly and he went down again, and Dave Wall wobbled around like a drunken man, not knowing that in thick, blurred tones he was reviling White and telling him to get up and take the rest of it.

Somebody had Dave Wall by the shoulder, pulling him back, talking to him. It was Cole Ashabaugh, and Cole was too strong to be pushed aside. He herded Wall to the bar.

"That's a big plenty, Dave. No use calling on him to get up . . . he can't. He's whipped complete and you're not doing so well yourself. Yeah, ease up and call it a day."

The support of the bar was good. Dave lay against it, his elbows hooked on it, his head bent while the effort of his labored breathing shook him all over. To Buck Sorenson and Pat Shea, Cole Ashabaugh ripped a sharp order.

"Get White on his feet and out of here. Clean him up a little first so folks won't think a murder has taken place. Mize, let's have your water bucket and a couple of bar towels."

The caressing chill of a wet bar towel was a benediction against Dave Wall's face and presently, when the effort of breathing was no longer a raw and salty rasp across his throat, a stiff three fingers of whiskey took hold and steadied him. He looked across the bar at Mize Callan.

"What's the damages?"

Callan shrugged. "One busted chair. Cheap ticket to a good show. But it's too bad you can't turn that kind of fighting ability to a better end, Wall." There was no slightest shade of friendliness in either the saloonkeeper's tone or glance.

"Mize," said Cole Ashabaugh, "you can be awful damn' thickheaded without half trying. By this time you should be thinking instead of just talking." The sheriff handed Wall his belt and gun. "There's a bunk over in my office,

Dave. Go use it for a while. I'll be over pretty quick."

Dave nodded wearily. "That listens good."

He cuffed his hat into shape, donned it, and walked out, apparently quite steady. But no one could guess how his belly muscles were shaking and how rubbery his legs felt. He'd left a lot of energy in that barroom.

Mize Callan stared at the empty doorway, then threw his hard glance at Ashabaugh. "So I'm a fool and I'm thickheaded. I talk when I should be thinking. Maybe you got another answer?"

"I think so." The sheriff nodded. "Would I have let that go on without good reason? You might have figured that, Mize."

"Why did you let it go on? With Wall being what he is . . ."

Ashabaugh cut in bluntly. "Dave Wall is a good man . . . a damn' good man. In his way bigger than you, Mize . . . bigger than me. Oren White's been asking for what he got for a long time. It's a lesson that could be applied to a lot of people. I'm hoping it sticks. Now here's a little story."

So then Cole Ashabaugh told the story and for some time after Mize Callan was silent. Then he reached for his private bottle.

"All right," he growled, "the drink's on me. I had no idea."

"A lot of people didn't," said Ashabaugh

mildly. "Including me. But now you know why Dave Wall worked for Lilavelt. You don't need to tell everybody the story, Mize, but you can sit on any loose talk you hear from now on."

The sheriff downed his drink, turned, and went out. At the office he found Dave Wall stretched on the bunk. He showed the sheriff a twisted grin. "That guy was tough, Cole."

"Showed more than I thought he had," agreed Ashabaugh. "He took a beating."

"He . . . and somebody else," murmured Wall. "Me."

Ashabaugh went over to his battered old desk, got out a pipe, loaded it, and puffed in silence, perching on a corner of the desk. "What worries me," he said abruptly, "is how things are going to stand now between you and Lilavelt, Dave. What do you intend to do?"

Wall stared up at the ceiling, his face slowly pulling into harsh lines. "Lilavelt made me a promise . . . I made him one. His was that the day I jumped the traces and refused to do any more of his dirty work, he'd expose Jerry Connell. Mine was that when and if he did that . . . I'd kill him." Wall stirred restlessly and his voice went cold. "Lilavelt kept his promise."

Puffing hard at his pipe, Cole Ashabaugh got off the desk, took a couple of turns up and down the length of the office. "It can't be as simple as that, man."

"Put yourself in my place, Cole," said Wall. "A damned dirty side-winder gets a club over your head. He really steals four good years of your life. He makes a dog out of you. He drives you into a spot where your friends turn away from you. He robs you of your good name, makes a damned pariah out of you. He's set to ruin the lives of those who mean most to you in the world . . . your only sister, her husband, and three little kids. Well . . . ?"

"Sure," said Ashabaugh quietly, "I know exactly what you mean. I'd feel just like you do. I'd want to walk him into a corner and fill him full of buckshot. I'll even agree . . . privately, of course . . . that he has it coming to him. But you can't do it, Dave. I'll tell you why. In the first place, it would be murder, for Luke Lilavelt would never go for a gun against you, and so give you the out of an even break. And so, I'd have to arrest you for murder." The sheriff tamped his pipe more firmly, scratched a freshening match. "Admitting that Luke Lilavelt is about as unsavory as they come, the cold fact remains, Dave, that the man cuts a big figure in some ways and some places. He's got money and property and power and those things reach far. And while there are no doubt some others who work for him who don't like him any better than you do, it's likewise true that he's got plenty on his payrolls who'd ride a long way with him.

His affairs wouldn't prosper as they have if that wasn't true."

Wall, remembering Nick Karnes and Whitey Brewer, Joe Muir and Hippo Dell, nodded. "You're right there, Cole . . . he's got that kind with him. But after he was dead . . ."

"They'd raise hell and put a rock under it," said the sheriff bluntly. "Oh, in time his organization, minus its head, would fall apart. But before it did, it could hit out plenty wild in a lot of directions and hurt a lot of innocent people. Here's another angle. Politics. Nothing is more cold-blooded. There are men up at the state capital who got there and who stay there because of votes that Luke Lilavelt has been able to deliver at the proper time and place. How would they feel if you knocked a prop from under them? Man, would they be screaming for your neck."

"Let 'em," rapped Wall. "Hell with 'em."

"And finally," went on Cole Ashabaugh evenly, "is the most important thing of all. Right now I've got your brother-in-law, Jerry Connell, locked up, facing a couple of damn' stiff charges. Let's not fool ourselves there, Dave. Oh, I know that Judge Masterson is going to do all he can for Jerry . . . and he can do a lot. Still and all, I'd hate to have to bet a leg on how Jerry's affair will come out. But I do know this. You go gunning for Luke Lilavelt right now and you'll hurt instead of help Jerry's chances. Better think on that, Dave."

Wall did think on it and with blinding abruptness he realized that Cole Ashabaugh was speaking the cold and bitter truth. "Damn you, Cole," he muttered. "You've taken my gun right away from me. And after waiting so long . . ."

Cole Ashabaugh drew a deep breath of relief. He knocked the dottle from his pipe and tossed it back into the desk drawer. "The last deal Lilavelt sent you on . . . that was the one you gagged on, wasn't it? Something about it that made you kick over the traces? Why?"

Wall was silent for a time, brooding. Then he began speaking slowly, and he told the sheriff the whole story of the affair in the Crimson Hills country. He told of Bart Sutton and the Square S and what he was convinced Lilavelt intended toward Sutton. He told of the shoot-out in The Rialto in Crater City, and how and why Nick Karnes and Whitey Brewer had died. "So that was it, Cole," he ended. "I downed Karnes and Sutton killed Brewer. Bart Sutton is a damned fine man. I just couldn't go against him. When I saw how it was in The Rialto, there wasn't the slightest doubt in my mind which way to move. I gunned Karnes so that Bart Sutton might live. That was where I was all done with Lilavelt."

"Things happen," said Ashabaugh, "that I don't

even hear about, it seems. Well, it's a damn' big county and I can't be everywhere. At best I can only hope to keep the lid on fairly tight. Do you think that Lilavelt will go on trying for Sutton's hide, anyhow?"

Wall considered for a moment, then nodded. "I think so. He can hardly afford to back out now. If he did pull away, why then a lot of others riding for him . . . men of the same stripe as Karnes and Brewer were . . . would begin to wonder. They'd begin to figure that in a tight pinch, Lilavelt wouldn't back them up. That kind of thinking would weaken the Window Sash organization all down the line. Lilavelt is smart and foxy enough to realize that. So . . . he'll keep on after Sutton."

"All right," said Ashabaugh. "You want to fight Lilavelt. There's your chance . . . the chance to hit at him and still be in the clear. Go tie in with Sutton. Get on the right side. And if Luke Lilavelt gets his ears shot off while trying to hog another man's range, then that's his hard luck, and there can be no come-back at anybody."

Dave Wall threw his legs off the bunk and sat up. A hard shine was in his eyes. "Cole," he said, "with your head, you ought to be governor."

Chapter Six

When Dave Wall rode out to the Connell Ranch he found his sister elbows deep in the snowy suds of a washtub. She came hurrying over to him, drying her hands on her apron. Her face was pale, her eyes big with worry.

"Jerry . . . where is he, Dave?"

Wall stepped from the saddle, put an arm about her shoulders. "Locked up," he said quietly. "It's for the best, old girl . . . and I'll tell you why."

As they walked slowly over to the wash bench, he told her. He told her about Judge Masterson and all that had taken place in the judge's office. "The judge is on our side, Judy, and he's going to do his best by Jerry. But he's right about sticking strictly to the law in trying to clear Jerry. It's the only way to settle this thing finally and for good. Once Jerry is cleared by the law, then it's a clear trail for him and you and the kids. And that's what we all want, isn't it?"

Judith sat on the end of the bench, beside her tub full of wash, and her shoulders drooped and her lips puckered and trembled and two big tears ran down her cheeks. At the moment she looked like a forlorn, scared little girl. She choked a little.

"B-But Jerry . . . my Jerry . . . in jail. . . ."

"It's still for the best," Wall comforted. "He'll live like a king and you can go visit him any time you want. But don't you see that Judge Masterson couldn't do anything else without advertising where his sympathies lay? This thing is going to take a little time and during that time we've got to keep Luke Lilavelt fooled. Suppose Judge Masterson had let Jerry go on his own recognizance, say . . . what do you think Lilavelt would think of that? I know. Lilavelt would set up an awful howl and stir up a lot of talk and feeling that wouldn't do Jerry's case a bit of good. No, it's better this way."

"What about the ranch . . . the cattle . . . the work to be done?" argued Judith. "I'll try . . . but I can't take care of everything."

"That's taken care of. Holt Ashabaugh will be riding out this afternoon. He's a good, dependable man. He'll keep the work up and keep an eye on you and the kids, too."

Judith began to flare. "If he's anything like his brother Cole . . . I'd rather not have him around. That Cole . . . arresting Jerry . . . !"

Wall laughed softly. "Don't you go throwing rocks at Cole, Judy. He's a good sheriff and a friend of ours, as you'll find out."

She considered this for a moment, then said: "If you're bringing Holt Ashabaugh out here to run the ranch, that means you're not going to be around, Dave. Where are you going?"

"Back to the Crimson Hills country for a time. Got business up there. Oh, I'll keep in touch with you . . . I'll write regularly. And you'll be able to reach me, general delivery, at Crater City. As soon as Judge Masterson gets some real developments on Jerry's case, I'll be right back here at your side, Judy."

She looked up at him. "Dave, you're positively all through with Luke Lilavelt?"

"Through working for him . . . but not through with him," said Wall grimly. "Before I'm through with him, he'll curse the day he ever heard the name of Wall."

Judith came to her feet, swift concern in her eyes, her fingers going up to touch Wall's lean jaw. "Dave. You're bruised . . . cut! Oh . . . I hadn't noticed. How . . . ?"

"Mister Oren White," explained Wall dryly. "For a long time his mouth has been too open. I shut it for him. Oh . . . he'll live. It was just a case of fists. But I think he learned his good lesson. And now . . . how about a little grub? I'm always hungry when I get near your cooking."

She wasn't to be put off this lightly. There was a fine and gentle sweetness in Judith Connell. "I know that Oren White has been making a lot of unfair talk, but it wasn't hurting anybody, really. Did you have to fight with him?"

"At the time it seemed like a good idea," said Wall slowly. "I think it did a lot more good than

123

harm. Besides . . ."—and here he grinned down at her—"your brother is a rough and ornery scoundrel. Didn't you know that, Judy?"

She surveyed him intently, then showed a small glimmer of a smile. "I wouldn't have him different."

While Judy got a meal together, Wall played with the twins, two sturdy little chaps, full of life and mischief. He went in for another look at the curly-headed little girl, still asleep in her cradle. And when he contrasted the warm, fine rightness of this little home against Luke Lilavelt's malignant cold-bloodedness, his hatred for the man rose dark and bleak within him.

When the meal was done, Wall went out to the saddle shed and fixed up a bunk there for Holt Ashabaugh, who came riding in, soon after. Like his brother Cole, Holt was tall and raw-boned. He was an impassive, slow-spoken man with steady blue eyes. He stowed his war bag under the bunk in the saddle shed, and while they put his horse away, Wall explained the situation briefly.

"Reckon I can take care of things to suit you, Dave," said Holt quietly. "Cole told me a few things when he rounded me up to come out here. You aim to put a few nicks in Luke Lilavelt's hide?"

"That's right, Holt. And, knowing the man, when he begins to smart a little, I wouldn't put it past him to hit back at me through this ranch.

You'll keep an eye open for that sort of thing?"

"Lilavelt wants his scrawny neck twisted, let him come out here and start something."

Holt Ashabaugh had never met Judy Connell, so Wall took him over to the ranch house and introduced him. Judy stood in the kitchen door, the twins clinging to her skirt, eying Holt soberly. Holt took off his battered hat with a quaint courtesy.

"Honored, ma'am. Any chore you want done, just holler." His glance went to the twins and a strange softness touched his leathery face. "Those little fellers . . . you think they'll friend up with me?"

He dropped on one knee, his slow grin touching the twins, who wriggled and squirmed, then suddenly dashed in and swarmed all over him. He hoisted one to each shoulder and walked up and down with them.

Wall met his sister's eyes and she nodded and smiled a little mistily. "He's a good man," she murmured. "Trust a child's instinct."

Wall set about his own preparations. He had a long way to ride and many things to do. He had the feeling of girding himself for a long, tough battle. But he was looking forward to it with an almost exultant eagerness. After those dark, stultifying years in Luke Lilavelt's besmirching service, with their hopelessness and morbid reactions, this was a great, fine freedom that he'd found. There was a new and eager energy in him and an astonishing sharpness of mind. It was as though a coating of rust and corrosion had been rubbed off, leaving the clean brightness of untarnished steel.

At parting, Judy clung to him briefly. "You'll be careful, Dave?" she entreated, a little choked up. "I know you wouldn't want me to hold you back, so I won't try. But it will be lonely and . . . and uncertain with both Jerry and you . . ." She reached up, kissed him, and pushed him away. "Good luck."

As before, Wall led a pack horse behind his saddle mount. His first intention had been to take to the desert again and ride directly for the Crimson Hills, but, after thinking matters over, he decided on a few other tactics. So his first stop was in Basin, for he wanted a final word with Jerry.

Cole Ashabaugh, loafing about his office, let Wall into the jail, where Jerry lay on a bunk, smoking endless cigarettes. "This," said Jerry, "is going to be tougher than I figured, Dave. Just this damned bubby and time, time . . . time! I'll go loco if Judge Masterson takes too long to get action of some kind."

"Think it's going to be easy on Judy?" reminded Wall. "This is something that just has to be taken and stood up to, cowboy. When Judy comes to see you, she'll have her chin up. Don't you let yours be dragging."

"I won't," promised Jerry. "Cole Ashabaugh says you got his brother Holt to keep the work up out at the ranch?"

Wall nodded. "And a damned good man, too. You won't have a single worry there. I stopped in here to let you know that."

Outside again, Dave Wall made another call at Luke Lilavelt's office, only to find it locked and silent and empty. His lips curled. Lilavelt, having loosed the law against Jerry Connell, had skinned out somewhere, afraid of the wrath of the man he had once held a club over.

When Wall went over to his horses, Cole Ashabaugh, who'd been watching from his office door, came sauntering up. "Not going back on our agreement, are you, Dave?"

"No. But I want to see Lilavelt. I want to tell him right to his teeth what I'm setting out to do. I want him to know that I'm going to start knocking the props out from under him, one by one. I want to make him start worrying, start losing sleep at night, put the fear of God into him. All that man has in the world, Cole, are his organization and his miserable, shrunken soul. I want him to know that I intend to smash up the first before I squeeze the life out of what's left."

"Ambitious chore," murmured the sheriff. "Will take considerable doing, my friend."

"Sounds like a big brag, doesn't it?" agreed

Wall. "But I'm going to take a man-size cut at making it good. Be seeing you."

Wall rode out of Basin, the hoofs of his horses chopping up a fine cloud of dust that made a tawny haze in the afternoon's westering sunlight. It was, he concluded, a pretty safe bet that he'd find Luke Lilavelt at one of his several cattle headquarters. Probably not at Crimson Hills, for that was a long ride and would serve no particular purpose at the moment. More likely, Lilavelt would be some place closer in, organizing for an all-out drive to the Crimson Hills, aiming to throw enough cattle and riders that way to start the big rollover of Bart Sutton and his Square S holdings. Lilavelt had mentioned Gravelly as the range where a herd was being gathered for the Crimson Hills drive, so perhaps that was where Lilavelt was now. Dave Wall headed for Gravelly.

Early dark found him on the flats along Powder Creek, so he threw his camp there, cooked his small supper, and, after eating, lounged on his blankets and watched the fire gutter out until the last ruby-red coal had turned to gray ash. The night world was big and still and the stars sifted down a moist coolness to freshen and sweeten all the land.

Dave Wall thought of other solitary nights along this trail or that, when riding to the orders of Luke Lilavelt. There had been no savor to most of them—they were just pauses to rest and eat and carried no significance beyond that. But this was different. A shadow had lifted from him, letting in a newly found freedom that had alerted all his senses of appreciation once more. And he found himself reveling in the simple gifts of life.

The small song of the chuckling creek waters, the stamp of a hoof and the champ of jaws as his horses foraged lazily under the stars. The shrilling of the tree crickets, the boom of a bullfrog from some backwater upcreek, and the lonely, rolling hoot of an owl from some gaunt sycamore top. Little things, common things, the breath of a land and the things that lived on or above it. Things that cost nothing, but which filled a man's cup to full and running over, when he was free to treasure them. . . .

At midmorning, Dave Wall rode up to Luke Lilavelt's Gravelly headquarters. It lay at the head of a small basin in a grassland of rolling, rounded ridges. A rich property, well watered, and well below the arid touch of the desert that lay to the north. Cattle grazed along the ridge tops and slopes and there was a faint stir of dust lifting to the north and east that indicated a considerable gather being thrown together up there.

Like all of Lilavelt's spreads, Gravelly had been held down to the barest essentials in buildings, and Wall thought again that there was no comfort for a man, either in his mind or his body, if he rode for Luke Lilavelt. Not if he was a man who in any way treasured his self-respect.

Wall came up slowly past the corrals and thought the place empty of life until Cube Spayd, the Gravelly foreman, came out of the bunk-house. Spayd was a short, powerful, and broad man, heavy-featured. He came over toward Wall at a heavy, stolid walk, showing neither surprise, welcome, nor any other animate expression.

Wall had never liked Cube Spayd, though he had worked with him several times. There was a large chunk of the crass brute in Spayd, and he would carry out any order of Luke Lilavelt's with a thorough ruthlessness. There was no conscience in this man, nor the slightest tinge of mercy for man or beast.

Dave Wall gave him a slow nod. "Lilavelt here, Spayd?"

"Was, but he's gone now," grunted Spayd, watching Wall with unwinking, dead-flat eyes.

"Where'd he head to?"

Spayd shrugged. "How would I know? He's always heading somewhere. What d'you want him for?"

"A little manner of business," Wall murmured. "Where's your crew?"

"Out gathering that herd we're to take up to the Crimson Hills. We'll be pulling out with it in a couple of days. You got that country open between Stinking Water and the Monuments? That was your chore, wasn't it?"

"Yeah," murmured Wall. "It was my chore." He put just the slightest emphasis on the word.

Cube Spayd had lifted his left hand and was scrubbing his black bristled chin with thumb and forefinger. His blank eyes flicked just the barest of glances at the bunkhouse door.

Abruptly every sense in Dave Wall's body was sharp and singing, shouting at him that something wasn't right about this set-up. Nothing was right about it, but everything was wrong. The place was too still, too empty. With that cattle gather going on to the north, Cube Spayd shouldn't be here—he should be out there supervising the job. For as Dave Wall knew him, Cube Spayd was a man very jealous of his authority, liking it and asserting it at all times. No, Cube Spayd shouldn't be here unless . . . !

Wall gathered his reins in his left hand, lifted them slightly. "Not like you, Spayd . . . to be loafing around headquarters, when there's a gather of selected critters going on. As I recall it, Lilavelt said the cattle were to be all two-year-olds. Who's out there picking them who can do a better job at it than you can?"

"No trick to that," Spayd growled. "Any damn' saddle hand halfway worth his salt can pick a two-year-old." Spayd's eyes were going harder and meaner by the second. "Reason I'm here is because we're expecting you."

He said this last swiftly, and he acted just as swiftly, bringing his left hand away from his face, down and back in a short, hard gesture that could be nothing else but a signal. And his right hand was streaking to his gun.

Before Cube Spayd's move was halfway through, Dave Wall was acting. His spurs drove home and he was reining up and hard to the left. Grunting and lunging under the bite of the steel, his horse whirled to the drag of the reins, smashing into Cube Spayd, knocking and spinning him to the ground.

Over at the bunkhouse door a rifle crashed sharply and Dave Wall clearly felt the heavy jar of the speeding slug. But it hadn't hit him and he kept his horse, whirling and rearing. He had drawn his gun when he first went into action and now it was poised, high and ready.

In the door of the bunkhouse a man stood, swinging the lever of a rifle as he pumped a fresh shell home. The man was Joe Muir, the rider who had slipped away from the Crimson Hills layout during the night after the shoot-out in Crater City, that had come so close to costing Bart Sutton's life.

Muir snapped closed the lever of his rifle and was whipping the weapon into line again. Dave Wall, coldly intent, drove a slug into the very center of Muir's body. Muir jackknifed and fell forward on his face like a man cut in half.

Cube Spayd, roaring with a sort of animal fury, was scrabbling around like a wounded bear, trying both to recover his jarred wits and the gun he had dropped when Wall's horse had smashed into him. Wall drove his frantic horse past Spayd, leaned far over, and chopped wickedly at Spayd's head with the heavy barrel of his gun. The blow landed, full and solid, and Spayd piled up in a heap.

Wall came fully erect in his saddle once more, setting his horse, while his bleak glance ripped the layout apart, watching for any slightest move of anything, anywhere. There was none, and Wall waited out the taut and stunned seconds.

Inside, he was coldly raging, mainly at himself for not guessing earlier that this was the sort of thing to expect. Luke Lilavelt had been here and had correctly figured that Dave Wall would also show. And Lilavelt had given the orders and planned the trap. And why it had not worked successfully, only the gods of chance knew.

Maybe Lilavelt was still here. Maybe he had waited to see Wall cut down, and then gloat over the fact. With the thought Wall sent his horse right up to the bunkhouse door. He didn't waste a glance at Joe Muir, who lay half in, half out of the doorway. When men went down like Muir had, they were done.

133

Wall swung from the saddle, stepped past Muir, had his look at the bunkhouse. It was empty. Back in the saddle again he swung up to the cook shack. There had been a Chinese cook at this headquarters. There still was, but the Oriental eyed Wall impassively over a pan of biscuit dough, showing no emotion at all, neither friendliness nor animosity. Evidently the cook felt that what happened beyond the door of his cook shack was of no concern to him.

Wall rapped: "Lilavelt? He here?"

The Chinaman shook his head. "He come . . . he go." That was all, except an Oriental shrug.

Wall rode back past Cube Spayd's sprawled figure. The man wasn't dead, but he'd really been hit and he wouldn't be taking much interest in things for a while. Wall took another look at that thin dust cloud. Whether the reports of the guns had carried that far he couldn't tell. But he knew that there was only one wise thing for him to do—which was to get away from this place and do it now.

His pack horse had been following freely behind him. Now he herded it out ahead of him, drove it to a full, swinging trot, and kept it going that way until he'd put a full mile and a couple of ridges between himself and the Gravelly headquarters. Here he paused long enough to get a scabbarded Winchester, which he'd had tied with his other gear on the pack horse, and sling the weapon under his near stirrup leather. When Cube Spayd got his senses back, there could be pursuit and in a case of that sort a man needed a long-range weapon close to hand.

Wall was still furious at himself. *You're a half-witted fool,* he told himself harshly. *You rode into that like some starry-eyed greenhorn and had more luck than you deserved, coming out with a whole skin.* He recalled the shock he had felt on the heels of the single rifle shot Joe Muir had gotten away. Where had it hit? Certainly not him and his horse was full of vigor. He ran an exploring hand over his saddle, and along the back of the cantle his fingers encountered a long gouge of torn leather.

That close had Muir come to getting him. Only that first forward and whirling lunge of his horse when he'd driven it into Cube Spayd had saved him. Only a few inches from a mortal body wound or savagely crippled hips.

Yes, that was the sort of thing Luke Lilavelt had cooked up for him. Other than at Lilavelt's orders there was no good reason why either Muir or Cube Spayd would have wanted his skin. Dislike him they might have, and probably did, but there was a considerable distance between dislike and the throwing of a gun at a man. Maybe Joe Muir had been playing with the idea of getting even with him because of Nick Karnes and Whitey Brewer, but Cube Spayd wouldn't have been influenced by that, and in the deal just finished back at Gravelly, Spayd and Muir had tried to work the thing together. So it had to be the hand of Luke Lilavelt behind it all.

The flaming anger had begun to die out in Dave Wall, replaced by a dark and forbidding grimness. This was the sort of thing he could now expect at any time and place where he met up with any of Lilavelt's Window Sash riders. Lilavelt would see to it that the word would go out. Get Dave Wall. That was the way it would be. Maybe in his anxiety to get Wall off the trail, Lilavelt would loosen up and lay out a little blood money—a reward for Wall's scalp.

In any case it meant that from now on he was a marked man, that he could trust few men thoroughly and most not at all. It would be a lone-wolf sort of trail. And also, as he had put it to Cole Ashabaugh, a dangerous trail.

For the next two hours Dave Wall kept his horses steadily at it, swinging well east, then north. Several times, on some higher crest of ground, he paused for a survey of his back trail, but nowhere could he pick up any sign of pursuit. After that he eased down on the pace, mindful of the long drag ahead.

He moved out of the rolling grass country and into the arid and hungry ground plain that bracketed the desert on the east. Just before sunset he found a trickle of brackish water in a badly eroded wash and set up there for the night. Around noon of the next day he rode into the town of Crater City.

He came in quietly and warily and found the place almost somnolent in the trapped heat under the lava rim. At a rickety livery barn he left his horses, with orders for a good rub-down and a big feed of hay and grain. Then he sought an eating house to feed his own clamoring stomach.

The place was small, just a single narrow room, with a counter reaching from side to side, faced by half a dozen long-legged stools. Beyond was a stove and a galvanized sink, several shelves of heavy-ware dishes, and a few cupboards. As the screen door closed behind Wall, a man came out of some shadowed depths beyond the stove. He was grizzled and gnarled and moved with a decided, swaying limp.

Wall perched on a stool and said: "Whatever is quick and easy."

Soon a steak was frying, and, as he watched over it, the crippled cook threw several glances at Wall. He slid the steak onto a plate, spooned boiled potatoes beside it, put this and a cup of coffee and a platter of bread in front of Wall. And now he spoke for the first time.

"Would you happen to be Dave Wall?"

Wall, mindful of the happenings at Gravelly and the necessity of continued vigilance, stared coldly. "I might be. And if so . . . what about it?"

137

The cook shrugged. "You got me wrong," he said mildly. "I'm not tryin' to pry. But if you are Wall, I thought you might be interested in seein' Tres Debley."

Wall was still, remembering now. That first night when he and Tres Debley rode into this town, Tres had said something about dropping in to chin for a while with an old sidekick who'd taken to running a hash house after being crippled up by a range accident. Wall recalled the name. "You're Charlie Ring?"

"That's right. Tres is out back. Eat your grub, and then I'll take you back to see him."

Wall's glance sharpened. "What's he doing back there, hiding? Man, you talk like something was wrong with him."

"There is," said Charlie Ring steadily. "He's all beat to hell. That fat cook, Hippo Dell, out at the Crimson Hills Window Sash layout, worked him over . . . plenty. Oh, go ahead and finish your meal. Tres'll keep. He's sleepin' a little now."

Wall, who had started to push away from the counter, settled back and began to eat. "When did all this take place?"

Charlie Ring spread his elbows on the counter, leaned there. "Yesterday afternoon sometime, I guess. All I know is that Tres come stumblin' in here just at dark last night, lookin' like he'd been mauled by a grizzly. I got him into a bunk and fixed him up as good as I could. He wasn't

138

altogether clear in his head, but he kept mumblin' somethin' about Hippo Dell, so I figured it must 'a' been Dell who'd been workin' on him. It was considerable past midnight before Tres quieted down and got to sleep an' he's been sleepin' ever since. I'm no sawbones, but I guess that's the best thing for Tres right now, plenty of sleep."

It was almost as though some invisible current stirred Tres Debley when Dave Wall moved into that back room with Charlie Ring and stood beside the bunk where Tres lay. For Tres, who had been so deep in sleep, gave a groaning sigh and pawed weakly at his face with a wavering hand.

A gusty, growling curse broke from Dave Wall's lips. In his time he'd seen some badly beaten men, but never anything like this. Tres Debley's face was almost unrecognizable. Everything seemed swollen to half again its normal size, just one great black and purple bruise. To all practical intent Tres was, for the time being, a blind man, his eyes hidden behind great rolls of bruised and beaten flesh. His lips were puffed and split and a three-inch cut across his forehead, just at the hairline, was freshly scabbed over.

"There ain't no doctor in this damn' town," said Charlie Ring. "But I did the best I could."

Dave Wall dropped a hand on Ring's shoulder. "Sure . . . sure you did, friend. Now I'll go to work. Bring me a bucket of hot water and half a dozen towels." He leaned low over the bunk. "Tres . . . how you feeling? This is Dave Wall, Tres. Take it easy. We're going to work some of the misery out of you."

Between putting one steaming hot compress after another on Tres Debley's face, Dave Wall examined the cowboy for other hurts. Tres was sound of arm and leg, but he bore bruises about his body where heavy blows had landed. Tres, fully awake now, drained a big dipper of water that Charlie Ring brought in and later did the same with a cup of coffee liberally spiked with whiskey. Then slowly, because his battered lips were clumsy at framing words, he told Dave Wall about it.

It had come out of a question of authority. Tres, left nominally in charge of Window Sash at Crimson Hills by Dave Wall, had issued a set of orders to Challis and Olds and Caraway, the three remaining riders. Hippo Dell, stepping out of his rôle as cook, had challenged these and given orders of his own. When Tres called him for it, Dell, without warning, had gone for him.

"He's fast, Dave," mumbled Tres, "faster than you'd ever believe a man his size could be. And strong . . . like a damned bear. I didn't have a chance to throw my gun. He took it away from me and then gave me what-for. It was like being hit by clubs when he threw his fists. I can't

140

remember much after the first time he hit me square. I know it was over, finally, and then there was somebody boosting me into my saddle. I think it was Harry Olds who was helping me. Sometime later I remember my horse coming down the lava rim above town, and I reckon it was more instinct than anything else that led me to this place of Charlie Ring's. Anyhow, that's it. Dave, don't you ever tangle with Hippo Dell . . . not hand to hand. Use a gun on him, or an axe, or a pick handle . . . but don't ever let him get hold of you solid. He ain't human at all, just animal."

Chapter Seven

It was dark when Dave Wall rode up to Bart Sutton's headquarters at Sweet Winds. While still a full hundred yards from the ranch house a hard challenge rapped at him from the dark.

"Far enough until I know you better! Who is it?"

"Dave Wall. I've got some words for Bart Sutton that he ought to know."

"Dave Wall . . . eh? That's Window Sash. Well, I got my orders from Bart Sutton to warm up the hide of any and all damn' Window Sash hands who come prowling. But you did give Bart a helping break not too long ago, so you get one more chance. Head out of here. Drift! And don't come back!"

Wall eyed the dark warily. "Suppose you take the word to Sutton? Tell him I'm here. Tell him I want to see him. I won't move from where I am until you get back. If Sutton doesn't care to talk to me, then I'll shove along. Use your head, man. I wouldn't be here if it wasn't serious."

"That's what you say," came the hard and wary answer. "But maybe I don't believe you."

"Oh, hell!" snorted Wall in sharp disgust. "Here . . . I'll give you my gun if you feel that way."

The guard was silent, considering. Then he said slowly: "All right. Stay put. I'll see what Bart has to say."

Wall heard him move off, presently glimpsed a rectangle of yellow light as a door opened and shut. After a short interval that same door opened and shut again, and then boot heels clumped and the guard was saying: "You win, Wall. Bart says for you to come on in."

It was Tracy Sutton who met Dave Wall at the door. She was in gingham, crisp and cool. Her hair shone in the lamplight. Wall stood silently, looking at her so steadily a slight flush grew in her cheeks. "It was Dad you wanted to see, wasn't it?" she asked pointedly.

"That's right. Didn't mean to stare. But you . . . startle a man."

Her color deepened as she led the way to her father's room. Sutton was sitting up, propped against pillows. He'd been reading. Now he eyed Dave Wall with some grimness. " 'Evening, Wall. Hardly expected Lilavelt to send one of his best men around to inquire about my good health."

There was that in Sutton's words and manner which puzzled Wall. A bitterness, a sarcasm, which certainly hadn't been there the last time he'd seen the man. Sutton seemed to read a different meaning in Wall's silence.

"Damn it, Wall," he burst out. "What kind of a man are you, anyhow? I thought, after the way you handled yourself in that affair in Crater City, that maybe your word in a matter was good. Maybe you didn't mean it that way, but I inferred that while you were in charge of Lilavelt's Crimson Hills layout, I could expect no further trouble there. I admit the idea was skimpy, what with you being Lilavelt's pet trouble-shooter and the guy who rolls the roughest of the rough stuff. But I still thought that . . . ah, well . . . wolf nature doesn't change, does it?" Bart Sutton tossed a resigned hand and reached for the pipe that lay on the table by his bedside.

Wall looked at him with steady gravity. "I don't know what you mean, Mister Sutton."

"I mean," snapped Sutton, "the kind of business that took place over on Soda Creek this morning." He fixed Wall with a brittle stare. "Maybe you've come to serve me with an ultimatum, after that."

Wall shook his head. "None of it adds up for me. You see, I've been away for several days . . . for as long as you've been in bed with that wounded side, in fact. I've been down across the desert, to Basin. I just got back today and I've been nowhere near Crimson Hills as yet. I stopped over in Crater City and didn't leave there until sundown. Just what did happen on Soda Creek?"

"One of my men, Sandy Carter, was line riding along Soda Creek. From the Window Sash side, somebody opened up on him with a rifle at long range. Without a shred of cause, without any purpose. But they meant business. They were really out to get Sandy. They killed his horse and shot a boot heel off Sandy while he was ducking for cover. And you know nothing about that, Mister Wall . . . nothing?"

A ripple of feeling moved across Wall's face. He turned toward the door. "Wasting your time and mine. If you don't believe me in one thing, then you won't in anything else. Sorry I bothered you."

Tracy Sutton barred his way from the room. She faced him steadily, very grave, her sober eyes taking in the smoldering bleakness of him. "Please," she said. Then to her father: "Dad, you're being very stupid."

"Stupid, am I?" barked Sutton. "What . . . oh, hell . . . maybe I am. Have a chair, Wall. Sorry. But being laid up this way takes all the balance out of a man. That and trying to figure out what makes a Lilavelt man do this or that. . . ."

"Suppose we get one thing straight," said Wall. "I'm not riding for Lilavelt any more."

Sutton reared up off his pillows. "Since when?"

"Since the second I threw my gun on Nick Karnes. No. Looking back, I can see that I was really decided on it before that."

Bart Sutton considered this, slowly lying back on the pillows again. "If that's the way things are, maybe you don't mind my asking why you've come back into this neck of the woods again? You see, Wall, I'm only trying to get things straight."

"So am I," said Wall. "For one thing I came to bring you word of something I think you'll be interested in. Lilavelt is bringing five hundred head of cattle in from Gravelly, aiming to drive between Stinking Water and the Monuments."

Sutton's eyes pinched down under frosty brows. "So the lightning is loose, eh? Held to that alone it wouldn't mean much. But Lilavelt won't stop there."

"No," Wall agreed, "he won't. If he gets away with that, he'll go on from there. He'll corner you if you let him."

Sutton's face went still with sober thought. "All my life I've wanted only to live at peace with other men . . . always figured that the world was big enough for all of us. I never could see where there was any percentage in trying to push the other fellow around or having him push me. I still feel that way, but, of course, if I have to, I'll fight for what's rightfully mine. Frankly I don't understand men like you, Wall . . . whose lives are geared to their guns. If you've broken with Lilavelt, as you say, and now bring me this word, it suggests that you want to hit back at Lilavelt through me. Am I right?"

Wall nodded. "Quite. I've considerable of an axe

to grind with Luke Lilavelt. And well . . ."—here he shrugged—"I don't want to see you pushed over."

"You feel no allegiance to Lilavelt because of your past connections?" probed Sutton.

Wall's lips twisted. "Hardly."

"I have never knowingly," said Sutton, "hired on a gunfighter to ride for me, and . . ."

"You're not hiring me," cut in Wall, the harshness once more deepening in his face. "You couldn't. I have something to say about that. Well, you now have the word I came by to give you. I'm glad to see you coming along . . . and I wish you luck."

This time he was out and gone before either Sutton or his daughter could stop him. They heard the ranch house door close behind him, and then silence settled over the room. Tracy moved over and sat on the edge of her father's bed. Sutton stirred restlessly.

"Damn it!" he burst out. "I suppose you're going to tell me again that I'm stupid?"

Tracy shook her head. "No, Dad. I don't know what to say. I can see your point . . . about not hiring him, I mean. After all, he is Dave Wall. After what he's been to Luke Lilavelt . . ." She went still again.

Sutton reached out, captured his daughter's hand. "We're in the man's debt, you and I. And there's a certain sincerity in him. Considering all

147

these things, it's hard to keep my judgment fair and clear. I appreciate the word he brought, and I'll act on it, of course. But I'd hate to feel that I was being used to satisfy one man's grudge against another. Youngster, this is a mixed-up state of affairs and I don't want to make any mistakes." He thought for a moment. "Go tell Spike Spears I want to see him."

He watched her as she went out. Everything that was worthwhile in life to Bart Sutton was tied up in this bright-haired daughter of his. Everything that he had built and amassed. And more—his hopes for her future. Watching her grow up, move into young womanhood, he pondered the day when some man would step up to claim her hand. A realist, he expected perfection in no man. But he did ask an honorable name and a reasonable promise of happiness for his girl.

As yet, he'd seen Tracy display no undue interest in any man until . . . He shook his head. It didn't add up or make sense. Probably it was Dave Wall's dark reputation that held a sort of macabre fascination for her young mind. Such things happened. A thoroughly bad man was always more interesting than a thoroughly good one. Or it could be that Tracy merely felt a sense of honest gratitude and obligation to Wall for what he had done for them. Or maybe he was just imagining things. . . .

He shifted, restless again, winced at the reminder his wounded side set up, then swore fumingly.

Dave Wall was not one to make the same mistake twice. At the Gravelly headquarters he'd come perilously close to being shot in half. Luke Lilavelt had given his orders there. Whether he'd been able to get the same kind of orders to the Crimson Hills by this time there was no way of telling. But it wouldn't pay to take chances.

There was a light in the bunkhouse, but the cook shack and cabin were dark. Wall left his horses some distance back in the night, and went in afoot. He scouted the surrounding blackness carefully before stealing up to a bunkhouse window and making a careful survey of the place.

A three-handed card game was going on. Olds, Challis, and Caraway were the players. Aside from them, as far as Wall could see, the bunkhouse was empty. Hippo Dell—where was he?

Wall stood for some little time outside the bunkhouse window. The three riders played like they were bored, disinterested, more or less sick of the company of each other. Wall moved on around to the bunkhouse door, which stood open. Alert for anything, he stepped swiftly in and to the side, putting his shoulders to the weathered planking beside the door.

The card players grunted with surprise, started to come to their feet, then settled back again as they recognized him. Wall rapped a cold query. "Dell . . . where is he?"

"Don't know," answered Olds. "In hell, I hope."

"You mean he's pulled out?"

Olds nodded. "This afternoon. Didn't say where he was going, didn't say when he'd be back. He took his war bag with him, so maybe he's gone for good. Which suits the rest of us right down to the ground. Not that it matters much, for unless things straighten out in this damn' layout and get to meaning something again, we're not going to be around much longer, either. We're about fed up."

"Fed up with what?"

"Everything." Olds was truculent. "Damn a job where nobody is boss, or if they are, they don't stick around long enough for a man to get used to them. This layout's been coming apart at the seams ever since Tom Burke left. Nobody else seems to give a damn, so why should we?" Olds kept meeting Wall's eyes stubbornly.

Wall grinned mirthlessly. "That's right . . . why should you? Any word come in from Lilavelt directly of late?"

"Not unless you bring it now."

Wall shook his head. "Lilavelt and I don't get along any more."

It was Challis who jerked a startled head. "You

150

mean you're not riding for Window Sash any more, Wall?"

"That's right. What about this mix-up between Tres Debley and Hippo Dell?"

"That," said Challis flatly, "was dirty. Hippo . . . he's a damn' animal. No man should ever try and mix it with him, hand to hand. A whiffletree or a pick handle is the medicine for Hippo."

"Or a slug," put in Caraway. "Dell ever starts after me, I throw a gun, for keeps. Tres Debley wasn't a bad sort. In fact, he's a pretty damn' good man. Made me sick to see what Dell did to him. Dell kept right on smashing him after Tres was cold as a wedge."

"You could," said Wall harshly, "have stopped it. Why didn't you?"

They stirred uncomfortably and Challis blurted: "You know how those things are, Wall. An affair between two men is their business. But when it got too bad, we did call Dell off, and he gave us a blistering cussing for it. But he knew better than to take on the three of us. Then we did what we could for Debley, put him on a horse, and headed him for town. We figgered it was best for Debley that we get him away from here entirely, else Hippo might have caught him alone again and finished the job."

Wall, seeing that there was no hostility in these men, relaxed and built a smoke. "There was a little affair of somebody trying to dry-gulch a

Square S rider out along Soda Creek. You fellows know anything about that?"

He could tell by their expressions that they did not. "News to us," declared Olds. "Don't know who could have tried that kind of a thing unless . . ."

"Unless . . . what?"

"Well," said Olds slowly, "after you left the last time you were here, Hippo Dell took to riding some. He had plenty to say about that affair in Crater City, when Nick Karnes and Whitey Brewer got theirs. I think he more or less blamed Tres Debley part way for that. Anyway, he quit living so much in the cook shack and took to riding. After seeing how he treated Debley, I wouldn't put it past him to dry-gulch a man . . . or anything else."

Wall nodded, sucking deeply on his cigarette.

Challis asked: "Where do we go from here, Wall . . . if anywhere?"

Wall shrugged. "Up to you . . . strictly. Understand that Lilavelt has got Cube Spayd bringing five hundred head of two-year-olds up from Gravelly. Maybe Spayd will get 'em here . . . maybe he won't. All I can promise is this. There's a rocky trail ahead for Luke Lilavelt and the Window Sash. Not only here, but at Gravelly, at Durbin Springs, at Pinnacle, Brockway Creek . . . everywhere he owns range, runs cattle."

"Don't get you," said Challis, startled. "Who's to cause the trouble?"

"I am, for one," said Wall flatly.

Challis considered this, eying Wall carefully. "I'm meaning no reflection, Wall . . . but I doubt you're big enough. A lot of chore for one man."

Wall smiled bleakly. "I won't be alone. I can think of a lot of men who've been tromped on at one time or another by Luke Lilavelt and who'd like nothing better than a chance to kick a spoke out of his wheel."

"That," admitted Challis, "is true enough."

Wall had moved to the door. "Think on it," he said briefly, before slipping out into the darkness.

The three men in the bunkhouse did not go on with their card game. They sat there, silent for a long time. Then it was Caraway who got up, went over to a bunk, dragged a war bag into sight, and began packing it with odds and ends of clothes and gear. "There's been the smell of something hanging over this layout for some time," he growled. "Now I think I know what it is. Luke Lilavelt's got too big for his britches . . . and in the wrong way. This layout is dying and I can't think of a single reason for staying on and dying with it. I've had a hunch for some time that I'd be wise to haul out. Now I'm going to. I don't owe Lilavelt a damned thing."

Olds stretched and stood up. "Jake, I think you got something there. Never stayed this long in one place before. Time to be moving."

Challis said: "Well, if you *hombres* think I'm

going to make a one-man stand of it, you're crazy."

Half an hour later Jake Caraway, Luke Challis, and Harry Olds rode away into the night. In the distance a Window Sash cow bawled forlornly, as though mourning a deserted headquarters.

Back in Crater City, Dave Wall put his horses in the livery corral, threw his blankets in the bed of an old freight wagon that stood nearby, and made a night of it. He lay for some time in thought. He was going to have to revise his original great plan. He wasn't going to be able to fight Lilavelt through Bart Sutton after all. The talk he'd had with Sutton this night showed that. At first a wave of bitterness ran over him, but on more sober consideration he realized that he couldn't blame Sutton for feeling as he did. He couldn't expect people to take him at face value as one kind of a man when he'd been, for so long, another kind. Maybe he'd never get out from under the stigma of having been Luke Lilavelt's toughest trouble-shooter. If he did, it was going to take a lot of time and a lot of proving.

Of course, maybe it would have been different with Sutton if he'd laid all his cards on the table, told Sutton the true story of why he'd been Lilavelt's man. But he instinctively shrank from this, either from a deeply ingrained sense of modesty, or equally deeply placed pride. He clung to the wish to prove himself in other ways, be accepted for his real qualities first, before letting that story out. Especially with Bart Sutton did he wish it so—and with Tracy Sutton.

He wished now that when he'd told Sutton that Cube Spayd would be bringing that herd up from Gravelly, he'd emphasized the fact that Spayd was a real tough one who'd be rough to handle, very rough. Wall hoped, if Sutton made any move to stop the herd, that he'd be smart enough to send a strong crew to handle a man-size chore.

The next morning, going into Charlie Ring's hash house, Wall found that Tres Debley had come back a long way after sound rest and reasonable care. The bruises still stood out, stark and cruel, on Tres's face, but a lot of the swelling had been reduced and so Tres could see out of both eyes and he was able to sit up and eat a fairly solid breakfast.

He showed a gargoyle grin to Wall. "I feel like hell and I know I look worse, Dave. But when you ride again, I ride with you."

"When I do, you will, cowboy," Wall answered. "But not today. Right where you are is right where you stay for at least another twenty-four hours. After that, we'll see. You hear, Charlie? This jigger stays put. Don't you let him out of bed."

Charlie Ring chuckled. "Agreed."

Charlie Ring went out front to tend to business and the grin faded from Tres Debley's beaten face. "You go out to Crimson Hills headquarters last night, Dave?"

"Yeah . . . I did."

"Hippo Dell . . . what did he have to say?"

Wall shook his head. "Dell wasn't there. Only Olds, Challis, and Caraway. According to them, Dell had packed a war bag, saddled a horse, and headed out somewhere."

"Good!" exclaimed Tres.

"Why good?"

"Because," said Tres with a slow, harsh emphasis, "I don't want you or anybody else getting at Hippo Dell before I do. That guy belongs to me, Dave. His trail is one I'm going to take and I stay with it until I come up with him. When I do . . ."

"You're a hard one to convince," mocked Wall mildly. "You asking for another mauling?"

"When I call Hippo Dell," said Tres quietly, "it'll be over a gun. Then we'll see."

"That's in the future," said Wall. "Lots of things in the future, Tres. Just now your chore is to get able to fork a saddle again. I'll stick around until you're up to it."

A good breakfast under his belt, Wall saddled up, left his pack horse in the livery corral, and headed out of town, riding south for several miles before swinging gradually over to where the dry plain and the desert joined and blended.

This direction he held to until nearly midday. His glance was roving and reaching continually ahead and in time he picked up what he was searching for—a long, low banner of dust.

It was many miles distant and to an untrained eye could not have been seen or, if it had, would probably have been taken for a quirk of the heat haze. But Wall read it correctly and a twenty-minute watch told him it was traveling north. The herd from Gravelly was on its way.

It was as he'd figured it would be. Cube Spayd, recovered from the gun-whipping Wall had dealt out, and knowing that the gloves were off, had reasoned that Wall would probably try and organize some sort of resistance to the movement of the herd. At best, he knew that Wall had already sided Bart Sutton against Luke Lilavelt's interests.

Spayd would decide that Wall would at least warn Sutton of the herd. So Spayd had thrown the herd into movement right away and was probably force-driving it, aiming to break through between the Monuments and Stinking Water before Sutton could build up enough resistance to stop it. Yeah, it looked like that was the way Cube Spayd had figured things.

Wall headed back to Crater City, riding in there at midafternoon. He put up his horse, had Charlie Ring cook up a delayed dinner for him, learned that Tres Debley was sleeping again. So then

Wall rolled a smoke, went over to the porch of the general store, took a round-backed chair there in the warm shade of the store's overhang, and settled down to kill the rest of the afternoon from this point of vantage where he could watch the street and all that went on along it.

Within an hour there was movement on the cutback trail down the face of the lava rim and Wall was startled to see Tracy Sutton riding into town. Trailing behind her was a grizzled rider leading a pack horse with an empty sawbuck saddle. Tracy was in blouse and divided skirt and her fair head was shadowed by a flat-brimmed Stetson. Wall liked her better that way than in jeans and admired her silently while she and the old cow-puncher rode up to the store and stopped.

Wall saw her glance swing his way, saw her slight start of surprise, and he touched the brim of his hat gravely and let it go at that. She and the old cowpuncher went into the store and presently the cowpuncher began moving in and out, lugging sacked flour and other grub staples that he slung to the led animal's pack saddle. He made up the pack expertly, covered it with a tarp, and threw a diamond hitch over all of it. Then he stood waiting, puffing a stubby pipe. Once or twice his glance touched Dave Wall, but he wasn't close enough for Wall to read any expression in it.

Presently Tracy Sutton came out, started to

leave the store porch, hesitated, and came over to Wall, who got to his feet and took off his hat. She eyed him with that grave soberness she'd shown the night before out at Square S headquarters.

"I hope you'll never think that my father and I are unappreciative of the favors you've done us, Dave Wall," she said simply. "I'm afraid you carried away an opposite opinion last evening, and I wanted you to know the truth of things."

"Sure," said Wall. "I understand. Now you heard me tell your father about a herd coming up from Gravelly. Well, I took a ride south of town along the edge of the desert this morning. That herd is on the move . . . it's coming in. I'd say it will reach that stretch between the Monuments and Stinking Water around noon tomorrow. So you tell your father that. Tell him this, too. That the man in charge of that herd is Cube Spayd, a rough, tough *hombre* who'll stop at nothing to break through . . . nothing. Tell your father to be prepared for that and not to send a boy out to do a man's job." His voice had become harsher while he spoke, but now it took on a gentler note. "I wish I could have given you better news than that."

She was studying his face intently while he spoke. "Thank you. I'll tell it to Dad just the way you've told it to me." And then she added impulsively: "How queerly fate can mix things up. There was a time when, to me, your shadow was a dark and frightening thing. But now I can see so plainly the deep strain of goodness that is in you. . . ." And then, as though overwhelmed by her own temerity, she flushed hotly, turned, and hurried to her horse.

Wall stood at the edge of the porch, a tall, sun-blackened figure, watching her ride away. He watched while riders and horses worked their way up the lava rim trail, and once, he was sure, she turned in her saddle and looked back.

That night Wall slept in the old freight wagon again, and when he went into Charlie Ring's place for breakfast, there was Tres Debley sitting on one of the counter stools, cradling a cup of coffee between his hands.

"Don't you holler at me, cowboy," said Tres. "I'm stiff as a sun-dried pine log, but I'm a whole man again and ready to go."

Wall took the stool beside him. "Ready to go where?"

"Wherever you go."

They traded glances and far back in the eyes of each a glint of understanding grew. "That," said Wall quietly, "I'm going to like."

They rode east out of town, facing the sun's morning sweep, their pace an easy jog, with Wall's pack horse shuffling along behind. Tres twisted and squirmed in the saddle under the loosening torment of his stiffened muscles, swearing softly now and then. But the growing warmth of the sun and the steady movement began to bring back some of the old suppleness and presently Tres was riding fairly easily.

"Thought you said something about taking Hippo Dell's trail and riding it to a finish?" jibed Wall, grinning.

"Where is Dell's trail?" retorted Tres. "You say he's pulled out of the Crimson Hills, so there's no use heading there. Besides, I'm not an old man. I got lots of time. But I would like to know where we're heading now."

"Basin," Wall told him. "But first I want to sit in and watch something."

Wall stood tall in his stirrups, swung his head, peering intently to the southeast. He lifted a long, pointing arm. "See it?"

Tres looked and saw. A long, lazy banner of dust in the distance. "What's under it, Dave?"

"Five hundred Window Sash critters. Aimed at forcing the gap between Stinking Water and the Monuments. Bart Sutton knows about it. We'll look on and see what happens."

They came in time to Soda Creek and turned south along it. Free of its drop from the Crimson Hills, Soda Creek became a sluggish, lazy stream, reaching ever farther south until, in the far, heat-hazed distance, it lost itself in a ragged smear of rusty green. This was Stinking Water, a bitter, alkali swamp on the edge of the desert where the waters of Soda Creek, which had started clear and cold and sweet far to the north, turned foul and died in slime-scummed sink-holes.

Some three miles to the west and a little farther north than Stinking Water lifted three gaunt, weathered spines of sandstone. These were the Monuments. The movement of the dust cloud indicated a line that would cut between the Monuments and the alkali swamp. This was the gateway of conflict for the Square S and Luke Lilavelt's Window Sash.

Dave Wall led the way to the far bank of Soda Creek, then pressed on toward the swamp. Sour willow and a kind of rank greasewood lined the creekbanks and behind the shelter of this Wall and Tres Debley rode. At a point approximately opposite the Monuments, Wall reined in.

"Let's find a chunk of shade, Tres. We got some time to kill."

They lounged in the thin shadow of a clump of willow, Wall propped on an elbow, Tres flat on his back, easing his muscles. Presently Tres stirred.

"When you pulled out at Crimson Hills after that Nick Karnes and Whitey Brewer affair, you said that while you were through with Luke Lilavelt in one way, you were just beginning with him in another. This part of it, Dave?"

Wall nodded. "If I hadn't felt completely that way before, I have since the Gravelly affair."

Tres came up sitting. "What Gravelly affair?"

162

Wall told about it, of the trap set for him at Gravelly, and how close his escape had been. "If you take a look at the cantle of my saddle, you'll see how close Joe Muir came to getting me," he ended. "Lilavelt ordered that, or Cube Spayd would never have been in on it. So if that's the way Lilavelt wants to play this game, that's the way it will be."

Tres marked the flinty cast to Wall's face and the sudden pinched-down chill in his eyes. He nodded. "Lilavelt's suffering right now, Dave. I never did know the man very well, only saw him a couple of times, in fact. Even so, I could see the greed sticking out all over him. And a greedy, self-centered *hombre* is seldom a brave one when the chips are down. He'll know by this time that his scheme didn't work, so I'll bet he hasn't had a good night's sleep since. He'll be seeing you in every shadow."

"Me, and a lot of other ghosts," growled Wall.

From time to time Wall got up, moved out to where he could look across to the Monuments and down to the approaching herd. By this time he could make out the dark mass of the cattle under the hovering banner of dust. They were coming on steadily, with no sign of opposition. He returned swearing.

"If Bart Sutton's going to do anything about this, he'd better get started. In another half hour that herd will be through the gap. What the devil's the matter with the man? I warned him, plenty."

"There's a reason," said Tres thoughtfully, "why men like Lilavelt so often trample better ones. The better man doesn't like violence. And then too often he hits half-heartedly instead of full out, because he feels that being in the right will fight most of his battle for him. Sounds good, but it doesn't always work out that way."

Wall built and smoked another cigarette, then went over to his horse and stepped into the saddle. "We'll leave the pack horse here and move in a little closer, Tres."

They went on downcreek another quarter of a mile and crossed to the west bank, holding there to the muffling outline of the willows. The Window Sash herd was coming remorselessly closer. Now it was possible to pick out the riders accompanying it, three at point, more along the flanks and in the drag. Maybe a dozen in all, a strong force, one that wouldn't be easy to handle.

"Lot of power in a herd of cattle," observed Tres. "Like a head of flood water, they can roll over and drown a man. Sutton better show his hand pretty quick, or he won't have any."

Wall did not answer, his lips pulled thin with bitterness. He might as well have saved his breath, it seemed, as far as Bart Sutton was concerned. But maybe he shouldn't blame Sutton too much. A fair man, thoughtful of the welfare of his men, maybe he felt he had no right to throw their lives on the line in an affair like this, where the issue added up to his own private gain or loss. Some men were big enough to feel that way and probably Sutton was like that . . . though mistakenly.

And then Tres Debley exclaimed sharply: "Over at the Monuments, Dave! There comes the Square S!"

Wall had been watching the herd. Now he swung his head. Lilliputian figures they were, at this distance and through the coiling distortion of sun haze, but mounted men beyond doubt, and moving down at an angle toward the point of the herd. But hardly enough of them for this chore. Wall watched for a moment, then looked at Tres.

"They're going to need help," he said briefly. "But this is no particular cause of yours."

Through his bruises Tres flushed. "The hell you say. Thought I told you that where you rode, I ride? Well, that's it."

Wall squared around in his saddle again. "We'll watch for a little and see how things shape up."

The gap between the point of the herd and the group of Square S riders closed. And then there were darting figures swinging out from the herd, massing and moving to meet the Square S contingent.

The two mounted groups held to close formation only for a little time as the distance closed between them. Then they began to spread and wheel and jockey for position and, though he could not pick up the reports at this distance, Dave Wall knew that rifles were beginning to bark out there, that the battle was joined, and that the invisible boots of Luke Lilavelt would be trampling out the blood of better men. It took only a moment to see that the superior force with the herd was getting the best of things. Almost immediately the Square S riders began to give ground.

Wall lifted his reins. "Come on, Tres!"

They went in at a hard run, angling toward the point of the herd, an idea taking form in Wall's mind as he rode. Two extra guns out in that tangled fight might make a difference, but again they might not. However, it was the herd that Window Sash was trying to put through, and if that herd could be turned!

The herd, with the weariness of a long drive in it, had slowed as soon as the pressure had drained away. The dust cloud caught up with it and settled down. Cube Spayd had left but four men with the herd, one at point, one on either flank, and one in the drag. The rest of his men he'd pulled off to meet the Square S attack. When the dust settled down about the point rider, bitter and shrouding, he cursed it and moved ahead blindly.

To Tres Debley, pounding along beside him, Dave Wall yelled: "Long chance, Tres! But we'll hit the point and see if we can turn it. That'll give Window Sash something to think about besides swapping lead with Sutton's crowd. All right with you?"

Tres's answer was to begin unstrapping the reata at his saddle fork.

There was just the faintest kind of small, hot breeze stirring, coming up from the south. It sifted the dust out in a long, saffron banner. Wall and Tres sped into this and it shrouded and hid them. The closer they got to the herd, the thicker the dust, until only a few yards was the limit of vision. The smell of the cattle and the sound of its steady bellow of protest against the weary miles rode with the dust. Wall held his loose-coiled reata in one hand, and when a steer suddenly loomed huge through the dust, he charged straight at it, flailing at it with the coils of his reata.

The animal whirled, plunged away, smashing into the others behind it. Then Wall, following, found cattle all around him, bellowing, surging, pushing back and to one side. Tres Debley, following Wall's example, added the pressure and persuasion of his own clubbing reata.

For a little time the pressure of the strung-out herd was too great to make any real impression on. It came pushing ahead, pushing ahead. But Wall and Tres kept fighting it, fighting a little at an angle instead of straight on. And gradually the animals immediately about them began to give to the side. Sensing this, Wall yelled thinly: "Stay with 'em, Tres!"

The point rider, blinded by the dust, had not seen Wall and Tres move in. But by now he knew that something was wrong. Cattle, instead of following him, were moving away from him, shifting to one side. He spun his horse, sent it lunging back through the dust. Abruptly he almost rode down Dave Wall.

The man had drawn his gun and he made a cursing, high-riding figure. There was nothing Wall could do but lash at him savagely with the hard coils of his reata. The blow landed, the hard-braided rawhide heavy and punishing across the fellow's head and face. It did two things. It spoiled utterly the direction of the shot the rider threw and it knocked him so far off balance that the sudden side swing of his horse, dodging to miss full collision with Wall's mount, spilled him out of the saddle. Wall raced on, the smell of powder smoke blending with that of dust in his nostrils.

The point of a herd was like the head of a snake—where it led the body must follow. And now, weary though it was, the point of the herd was knowing a growing panic. It was a catching fever, passing from one critter to another like fire sweeping dry grass.

Wall and Tres redoubled their efforts, half-strangled in the dust, yelling now and working those clubbing reatas until their arms grew numb and weary. But they had that point going, curving out in the start of a turn. A lead steer broke into a wild, crazy run, sucking another and still another with it. Racing on the outside of that curve, keeping even with it, Wall and Tres kept pressing, pressing, until, abruptly, they knew they had their gamble won.

The whole herd was in quickening movement now. The center body of the herd began to race after the fleeing point and the drag slashed after the rest. In its entirety it became a wide rough half circle of hurtling bovine flesh, of spouting, upsurging dust, the point leading back the way it had come, then veering left toward the desert and the poison bog holes and sinks of the Stinking Water swamp.

Wall pulled a little wide and stopped, Tres coming up beside him on his sweating, blowing horse. Tres was exultant. "That ought to worry somebody!" he yelled.

It did. The left flank rider, caught on the inside of that curving, blind river of cattle, had to ride for his life. The right flank rider and the one at the drag, lost in that fog of dust, charged helplessly about, not at all sure of the how and why of this, but knowing that something had gone radically against plan.

Out where the fight against the Square S riders was going on, a Window Sash hand raced in on

Cube Spayd, yelling wildly, jerking a violently indicative thumb over his shoulder. Spayd, blind to all else but the battle at hand, cursed the man out of the way, but when the fellow persisted, Spayd turned and looked and saw the herd streaming away.

Cube Spayd had bossed this drive, led it this far. He had, on seeing the Square S opposition appear, gone into battle with a savage, ruthless truculence and had seen the Square S forces give way and back up, slowly but definitely. He had known the exultation of what had been a winning fight. But the fight meant nothing unless the herd was put through. Now it was running— but the wrong way.

Spayd didn't know why or how it had come about, any more than did some of the wondering Square S men, but they did know that the pressure on them began immediately to let up, while Cube Spayd began yelling wildly at his men, splitting his force, sending some back after the herd, trying to rally the rest to press on in the fight.

So far, the fight had been at relatively long range. Even so, two Square S horses were down and a Square S rider was humped sickly in his saddle, dazed and reeling with a smashed shoulder. As yet Window Sash had suffered no casualties.

A Square S man levered another shot from a reeking Winchester. He had fired with no particular aim, using the whole shifting, dust-filmed mass of the enemy as a target. But he shot better than he knew. The bullet told with a sodden thump.

Men about Cube Spayd, men close to him, listening to his raging orders, saw him suddenly reel far back over his saddle cantle, where he seemed to hang, stiffly rigid, his face to the sky, his teeth bared, his voice dead in his throat. Then all substance seemed to pour out of him and he was a limp huddle, folding down the side of his horse and piling up on the ground.

It was a vital, breaking blow to Window Sash. The tough ruthlessness of the leadership that had brought them this far was gone, lying dead there on the hoof-trampled earth. The color of Luke Lilavelt's money wasn't enough to hold the rest of Window Sash to the chore. Had the herd still been coming steadily ahead they might have made a try at seeing the affair through, even with their leader gone. But the herd was careening away to the south and east and it was a stampede that built up panic and dragged defeated men with it.

They broke away in ones and twos and threes and soon only Cube Spayd remained, marking the high point of their advance. It was like a tide that had rolled so far, then broke on some invisible rock, and so flowed back, faster and faster.

Square S gathered its forces, counted its

casualties, then came ahead, measuring the battlefield with grim eyes. Out where the dust was clearing they saw two riders, sitting their horses quietly, showing neither hostility nor friendship. Four Square S men rode slowly over, rifles ready across their saddles. The leader of the four was a raw-boned, hard-jawed man with a bloodstain on one shirt sleeve. There was haggard fire in his eyes.

"Why don't you run like the rest?" he growled. "If you're aimin' to try and talk this thing out now, you're crazy. You started it . . . we'll finish it!"

Dave Wall said: "Before you go jumping at conclusions, ask yourself why that herd swapped ends and started to run. Not on its own account, friend."

The raw-boned rider started slightly and his stare was hard and searching. "Your voice . . . I heard it the other night when I was on guard at headquarters. You're Wall?"

"That's right. I told Sutton this herd would be coming in and offered to take a hand in fighting it back. He couldn't see it just that way. But Debley, here, and I took a cut at things anyhow. We figured if we could turn the herd and start it running while Cube Spayd and his crowd were busy holding you off, it would help some."

"Once you rode for Lilavelt, now you ride against him. Why?"

"We got our own good reasons."

The raw-boned rider nodded slowly. "Your business. Well, turning that herd helped all right . . . helped plenty. They were tough up to a point, and then all of a sudden they were done for." He pushed a hand across his face and slacked off a little in his saddle, a man drained dry by the short and savage fury of battle.

"Knowing Spayd," said Wall, "I wonder at him quitting so suddenly. He's a tough *hombre*."

One of the other Square S riders spoke up. "They broke right after one of their crowd went down. Maybe that was Spayd. What's he look like?"

"Tell you better when I see him," Wall said. "If you want it that way?"

The raw-boned rider reined about. "Come on."

They rode over and Dave Wall had his look. He nodded. "That's him, sure enough. Well, there's your answer. A hard man, riding a hard trail, come to a hard ending."

Wall built a cigarette, brooding a moment. Here was another ghost for Luke Lilavelt to remember. Wall shook himself and looked at the raw-boned rider. "If it's all the same to you, my partner and I'll be drifting."

The raw-boned man, friendlier now, shrugged. "Far as I'm concerned the trail's open. I'll see that Sutton hears about that herd being turned . . . and who did it. Good luck!"

Chapter Eight

Sheriff Cole Ashabaugh, lounging at ease in the doorway of his office, saw Dave Wall and a companion turn in at the lower end of Basin's street and come jogging along that hot and dusty way. As they pulled to a stop before him, he lifted a hand in greeting, marked the signs of far travel on riders and mounts, and tried without success to read the thoughts behind the weathered darkness of Wall's face.

Wall said: "Cole . . . howdy!" And then, before dismounting, put a long glance on Luke Lilavelt's office.

Ashabaugh said: "He's not in town, Dave. Hasn't been since you left. I've begun to wonder."

"Wonder what?" Wall stepped from his saddle and stamped some of the riding stiffness from his legs.

"Whether you haven't caught up with him somewhere and forgot to tell me about it?"

"No such luck," said Wall. "Shake hands with a good friend of mine . . . Tres Debley. Tres, this is Sheriff Cole Ashabaugh."

They had made the long ride down from the Crimson Hills country by easy stages and along the way Tres had lost virtually all the signs of his beating at the hands of Hippo Dell. He took Ashabaugh's hand with a quiet nod.

"How's Jerry making it?" asked Wall. "And any word from the south yet?"

"No word so far," informed the sheriff. "Jerry's healthy, but restless. You want to see him, I suppose?"

Ashabaugh gave Wall the jail key and Wall went in alone. Jerry Connell came to his feet eagerly. "Dave! Man . . . it's good to see you. What's the word?"

"Nothing yet. Tough ride, hey, feller?"

Jerry, going sober, nodded. "Plenty. Much more of this and I'll end up talking to myself. Been out to the ranch?"

"Not yet. Heading there when I leave here. Judith's been in to see you, of course?"

"Every other day. She's great, Dave. And I sit here thinking what a dog I am for getting her into this mess."

"None of that," rapped Wall sharply. "We made a bargain, all of us. We'll see it through." Then in a milder tone: "They can't keep you locked up here forever without taking some kind of direct action. Keep your chin up."

They talked for a little while, and then Wall left. Tres Debley was waiting for him in Ashabaugh's office. The sheriff, as he accepted his key back from Wall, drawled: "Before you leave, Dave . . . a couple of questions. Word leaked in from Lilavelt's Gravelly headquarters that a man had been killed out there . . . fellow named Muir. Know anything about that?"

"Yeah," answered Wall bluntly, "I know all about it. Come outside and I'll show you something."

He led the way to his horse and indicated the bullet-gouged cantle of his saddle. "That's where Muir's slug hit. And he had first bite." Then he sketched in the other angles of the Gravelly affair briefly. "How did the word reach you, Cole?"

The sheriff pulled a folded bit of paper from his shirt pocket, smoothed it out, and handed it over. "I found this shoved under my office door one morning."

It was a page that had been torn from a small notebook. On it was roughly printed with pencil a few words that read:

Ask Dave Wall what he knows about the killing of Joe Muir at Gravelly.

Wall's lip curled as he returned the paper. "Friend Lilavelt doesn't overlook a single angle, does he? I've seen him use a notebook about this size, plenty of times." He faced Ashabaugh grimly. "You've heard my story, Cole. What's the answer?"

The sheriff pocketed the paper again, shrugging. "You never were a liar, Dave. Your story suits me until somebody can prove different. If I can ever get you and Lilavelt face to face, maybe we'll reopen the question. If you're going out to the ranch, tell Holt that Henry Laramore has got another jag of saddle stuff he wants softened up. Maybe you can take over at the ranch long enough for Holt to keep Henry happy?"

"Can do," agreed Wall. "I'm sticking close to these parts now until something breaks in Jerry's trouble. Tres, shall we ride?"

For the next two weeks Dave Wall lived life as he had dreamed of it, back through the dark, grim, lonely years while riding the hard, trouble-shooting trails for Luke Lilavelt. He sent Holt Ashabaugh over to take care of Henry Laramore's job and he and Tres Debley tied into the ranch work. The big chore was the cutting and stacking of tons of wild hay, sun-dried and lush along the meadows of Magpie Creek. It was good to work with a freedom of spirit, to leave his guns off, and not have to be continually throwing the weight of his will and commanding purpose against sullen, hard, dangerous men. It was good to relax completely, mind and body, to let the sweat flow, with the sweetness of earth's growing bounty lifting to his nostrils. It was good to sit up to the warm, savory supper table and talk over the simple earthy problems of everyday ranch work at a slow leisure with Judith and Tres

Debley. It was good to have the twins skylarking about, to hear the small treble of their childish shouts, and to have them ride on the seat of the hay wagon with him.

Into this small circle of activity, Tres Debley fitted with a quiet, unassuming ease. Watching, Wall saw a new content settle in the wind- and sun-puckered eyes of lean, dependable Tres. And one day Tres said: "This is the way the Lord intended a man should live, Dave. For all these years I've chased up one trail and down another, never knowing exactly what it was I hoped to find, yet knowing I'd never be content until I did. And right here, all about me, is what I've been looking for."

Judith, thought Wall, was a champion, all right. Regularly she went into town to see Jerry, always taking with her some tasty dish she'd cooked especially. Proud she was, as she had always been, and now she showed her pride by being faithful through everything to the man of her heart. Wall knew that secretly she was undergoing a lot of punishment, but she kept it well to herself. Outwardly she was cheerful and smiling. But more than once Wall saw her furtively wiping her eyes after putting her small brood to bed for the night.

Wall would have liked to comfort her, but he was wise enough to know that words of sympathy wouldn't help at all. This was something that just had to be wearied out.

And then, one evening, Sheriff Cole Ashabaugh rode out. "Word's come up from the south concerning Jerry," he told Wall. "Judge Masterson wants to see you, Dave. Tonight."

"Good or bad word, Cole?" asked Wall tautly.

"Not rightly sure," said Ashabaugh slowly. "Kinda depends on how long and far a man can hate, I guess."

Wall buckled on his guns and drew Tres Debley aside. "Keep an eye on things, cowboy. This trail is only beginning to open up. And you're riding it with me. That's a promise."

"I'll be here," nodded Tres. "When you want me . . . holler."

There was a tall, ramrod-straight man with grizzled hair and a bitter, hawkish face with Judge Masterson when Dave Wall and Cole Ashabaugh clanked into the judge's office. There was a faint air of tension and hostility in the atmosphere and in the yellow glow of the lamplight. Wall thought Judge Masterson looked more stern than he'd ever seen him.

The judge shook hands and then said brusquely: "Meet John Ogden. Mister Ogden, this is Dave Wall, brother-in-law of Jerry Connell."

John Ogden made no attempt to shake hands. Gray, stern, relentless eyes burned at Wall, who murmured: "Ogden! The town marshal of Round Mountain was named Ogden."

"My son," said John Ogden harshly. "And he

was shot down like a dog in performance of his duty. Shot down by a crowd of drunken, worthless thieves and hold-up men. Considerable years ago that happened. But I haven't forgotten or forgiven, and I never will. I've dedicated every dollar I own and all the balance of my life to bringing to justice the killers of my son. It seems that at last the law has caught up with one of them. I've come up here from New Mexico to arrange for extradition. I want this fellow Connell back at the scene of the crime where I can go to work on him. I'm telling you this, Mister Wall, so you'll have no false ideas as to exactly where I stand and what I propose to do. This Connell may be your brother-in-law, but Charles Ogden was my son."

A cold current ran up Dave Wall's spine. If he had ever listened to a man's inflexible, cold, unalterable determination to exact vengeance, he was listening to it now. He searched John Ogden's face and could find no slightest sign of mercy in that bitter, hawkish visage. A little desperately he said: "Jerry Connell did not kill your son, Mister Ogden. Jerry never fired a shot. The shooting was done by a man named Big George Yearly."

John Ogden made a harsh, dismissing gesture. "So you say. But you don't deny that Connell was one of the gang?"

Wall turned to Judge Masterson. "Have you told

the entire story to Mister Ogden as Jerry gave it to you, sir?"

"I've sketched the high points, no more," answered the judge. "I think perhaps it might be well to have Jerry tell it himself. Sheriff Ashabaugh, will you bring Mister Connell here?"

Cole Ashabaugh went out. Dave Wall built a cigarette, trying to fight back the panic in him. This sort of thing was the last he dreamed would happen—not a man as cold and inflexible as this one, bound on vengeance.

Not another word was spoken in Judge Masterson's office until Cole Ashabaugh returned with Jerry. The moment Jerry came through the door, John Ogden fixed him with a cold, implacable stare.

Quietly Judge Masterson explained matters to Jerry. Then he added: "Will you give us your story again, Mister Connell . . . exactly as it happened?"

Jerry faced John Ogden and gave it, simply and quietly. But when Jerry finished, there was no slightest break in Ogden's manner or expression.

"You were one of them," was Ogden's harsh comment. "You were an accessory. In my eyes every man in that gang was equally guilty. Judge Masterson, I demand that we get along swiftly with the matter of extradition. Aside from that there is nothing more to say."

Judge Masterson steepled his fingers, pursed his lips, and his eyes took on a cool glint. "On the contrary, Mister Ogden . . . there is much more to be said. I have told you about Mister Connell's excellent reputation hereabouts. I've told you of his record of hard work, reliability, and accomplishment. I've told you of his local reputation as a solid, law-abiding, desirable citizen. I wanted you to hear his own story from his own lips. I also told you about his fine family, his wife and children. I had hoped all these things would have some effect upon your judgment and generosity. Apparently there has been no effect." The judge paused, sat a little straighter in his chair. "I can sympathize fully with your natural grief at the death of your son, but the fact remains that Mister Connell did not fire the fatal shot . . . he did no shooting at all."

"So he claims," rapped John Ogden. "He could be lying and probably is."

"I choose to believe otherwise," said Judge Masterson. "I believe that Mister Connell has given us the exact truth of that affair. Oh, I admit to your premise that he stands accessory before the law. But true justice, Mister Ogden, is always tempered with understanding mercy. You, apparently, do not feel that way. So you leave me with but one alternative. If you refuse utterly to view this thing in a more fair and generous light . . . if you persist in your demands for immediate extradition, then, sir, I must warn you that you are in for the fight of your life."

Judge Masterson got to his feet, spread his hands on his desk, and leaned forward with a startling belligerency. "I can, Mister Ogden . . . and I will, dig up delays and points of law until you choke on them, sir. You are fighting for the memory of a dead son, riding a malevolent vengeance that hardly becomes a man of your age. While I am fighting for the rights of a living man, for the happiness and future of his family. If I had the slightest feeling that Jerry Connell had contributed directly in the murder of your son, I would hand him over to you without a word. But I do not feel that way. So, sir . . . do we talk this over in a new and understanding light, or is it to be a battle?" The judge's eyes had locked with those of John Ogden and for a long moment the clash of wills hung, hard and inflexible. It was Ogden who finally looked away. Then the judge said, his voice growing mellow again: "The man who killed your son, Mister Ogden, was named Yearly. Known as Big George Yearly. He was the leading sinister influence in the whole affair. Why not concentrate your efforts in running him to earth?"

"I have made that effort and I'm continuing it," growled Ogden. "The fellow seems to have dropped completely from sight. However, I intend to continue my efforts until I locate him or know beyond doubt that he is dead. As for the custody of this fellow, Connell, there you shall have your fight, Judge Masterson. I haven't gone as far as I have on this issue to back away from it because of a fight. You'll hear from me, make up your mind to that."

Ogden whirled, put another hard and measuring stare on Jerry Connell, then stamped out.

Judge Masterson looked at the empty doorway for a long moment. Then he murmured: "That man is to be pitied. He's eating himself up with a black obsession."

Dave Wall took a short turn up and down the room. "How long can you hope to hold up extradition, Judge?"

The judge settled slowly back into his chair, as though a little weary. "Not as long as I'd like to, I'm afraid. Part of my recent defiance was sheer bluff and I'm afraid John Ogden knows it. Oh, I can win some delay. A few weeks, maybe a month. But that is all. If there was only some chance of locating this Big George Yearly and rounding him up. Could we put the actual killer of his son before John Ogden, that might solve everything for us."

"After all these years I'd call it almost an impossibility to locate Yearly," said Jerry Connell dully. "For all we know, Yearly could be dead. Judge, you've been mighty fine about this, but it looks like . . . well . . ." Jerry shrugged a little hopelessly.

Dave Wall looked at his brother-in-law. Jerry's shoulders were slumped and he was staring straight ahead, as though seeing nothing but black shadows. The fight, thought Wall grimly, was going out of Jerry.

Cole Ashabaugh cleared his throat. "Mind if I put in my two-bits' worth, Judge? To me there is one angle of this affair that don't add up right. Me, I've been wondering how Luke Lilavelt got hold of that Wanted dodger on Jerry in the first place. Lilavelt is a cowman and in the general run of things would have no reason at all to be interested in anything like that. Particularly a dodger from out of state. Yet he turns up with this one on Connell. How and where did he get it?"

A gleam came into Judge Masterson's eye. "Sheriff," he murmured, "that's using your head. Go on, man. Where else does your thinking lead you?"

Ashabaugh turned to Jerry. "If I remember right, you said that Yearly and three others went into that deadfall at Round Mountain and that only Yearly came out alive. In which case, only you and Yearly lived through the mix-up. That's the way it was?"

"Yes," said Jerry, slightly wondering, "that's the way it was, Cole. But what . . . ?"

"Supposing," cut in Ashabaugh, "that I'm Big

George Yearly. I'm on the dodge for killing a town marshal. Riding on my shoulder all the time is the realization and the fear that someday, somewhere, I'm going to be picked up. I'm drifting here, drifting there, covering up my trail. One day by chance I happen to run across the only other living member of the gang who was in the mix-up. He doesn't see me, but I'm dead sure of him. That man hadn't had much to do with the affair. He wasn't actually in on the attempted hold-up, and he didn't do any shooting. But he knows that I'm the one who killed the town marshal. In a court of law he's the one witness who could actually put a rope around my neck." Cole Ashabaugh paused, built a cigarette, then went on. "While that man lived, he would be mighty dangerous to me. But to kill him would open the trail again, hotter than ever, for by now he's a family man, a ranch owner, and a man in good standing in his particular neighborhood. But if I found a way to tip the law off about him without showing myself in the picture, then the law could gather him in and prosecute him and maybe that would satisfy the law and leave it not near so anxious after my skin. At any rate, he'd go over the road even if he wasn't hung, and with him out of circulation there'd be no chance of him seeing and recognizing me, and by turning state's evidence on me, get off easy himself. Is that kind of thinking too far-fetched, Judge?"

Judge Masterson, his eyes pinched down, considered for a time in silence. Then he shook his head. "No, Sheriff . . . not too far-fetched at all. It makes sense. It is logical. Over the years I've seen the truth arrived at through premises built up on far sketchier foundations than that. That fear, which always rides with the guilty, causes them to do strange things. More than one culprit who, as far as the law is concerned, has dropped completely from sight and been virtually forgotten, has betrayed himself by some move calculated to cover a trail more thoroughly that has already dimmed out to nothing. Why shouldn't Big George Yearly make the same mistake?"

Cole Ashabaugh nodded. "That's clearing it up, Judge."

"The big point, of course," said the judge, "is that Luke Lilavelt could have some idea of the present whereabouts of Big George Yearly . . . that it was Yearly who put the dodger in Lilavelt's hands?"

"Right," affirmed Ashabaugh. "Yearly could easily have got hold of such a dodger. Lots of times they're posted in public places. For that matter, I've known of outlaws who were packing around a dodger concerning themselves when picked up. The mind of a hunted man can cook up some queer twists."

The judge stirred briskly. "Right or wrong, this

187

line of reasoning at least gives us something to go on. Sheriff, I want Luke Lilavelt brought before me. I want to ask that man some very pointed questions."

"He may not be easy to find," said Ashabaugh slowly. "He left town the night before I went after Jerry with that warrant and I haven't seen him since. I know his office has stayed locked up, and when I checked at the room he keeps in the hotel, that hasn't been used, either. But I'll sure start looking for him."

Dave Wall had been a silent but intent listener. Now he spoke up. "I don't think that would be the right move, Cole . . . your going looking for Lilavelt, I mean. Because you're the known law. The word goes out that you're trying to locate Lilavelt, and Yearly, if he is somewhere in these parts, he might spook and pull out. It's the law he's afraid and suspicious of, remember. On the other hand, if I'm looking for Lilavelt, that would shape up as a personal angle between Lilavelt and me, and Yearly would have no cause to get too excited over it. Besides, I know Luke Lilavelt better than any other man. I know how his mind works. I know all his spreads and how the trails run. Let me go after Lilavelt . . . let me bring him in."

"Why now," exclaimed Judge Masterson, "that is clear thinking, too, Mister Wall! And there would be a sort of sublime justice in it, all things considered. I think you're right. Sheriff, I suggest we put Wall on the trail . . . er . . . slightly irregular, I admit . . . but this is a case that demands emergency measures."

Cole Ashabaugh put a long glance on Dave Wall. "Understand, killing Lilavelt wouldn't solve anything, Dave. We got to have him able to talk."

"Clear enough," assented Wall.

"All right," said the sheriff. "If it suits the judge, it suits me."

It was close to midnight when Dave Wall got back to the ranch. Everything was dark. Wall quietly put up his horse, then went over to the saddle shed where Tres Debley bunked, and shook him awake. He told Tres all that had taken place in Judge Masterson's office.

"This changes our plans some, cowboy. You'll have to stick on here until Holt Ashabaugh gets through with his chore for Henry Laramore and comes back here," Wall ended. "I'll try and keep in touch with you. I don't know how long and far I'll have to ride to locate Lilavelt. One thing is certain. He's got to be around somewhere. He can't afford to stay out of sight too long and let all his business interests go to pot."

Tres said: "I'll stick until Ashabaugh gets back. Then I'll do some riding myself. Probably back into the Crimson Hills. For I got a guy I want to find, too, remember. Hippo Dell. I owe that *hombre* a going over with a pick handle and I won't be happy until I pay that debt. The Crimson Hills is Dell's country, so that's where I start looking. Maybe by this time he's back at the old headquarters."

"He's a tough one," reminded Wall. "You should remember that."

A ripple of remembered feeling pulled Tres's lips thin. "Next time it'll be different," he said with some harshness.

Chapter Nine

For the next two weeks, Dave Wall rode more miles than ever before in his life during an equal period of time. All were trails he had covered before in the service of Luke Lilavelt, but never at such a driving, unrelenting pace as now. He left gaunted, weary horses behind him and drove ahead on fresh ones. He rode himself down to sheer rawhide and sinew, while sun and wind burned him black. And he rode with a bright and brittle alertness at all times, for each one of Luke Lilavelt's far-flung cattle headquarters could be a deathtrap for him under Lilavelt's orders.

Anywhere along the trail some Window Sash rider, for the sake of a few extra dollars, could be watching and waiting for him, a rifle always ready. There were, he thought grimly, quite a few like Joe Muir on Luke Lilavelt's payroll. On the other hand, there were also men like Tom Burke and Tres Debley. Men with a restless, perhaps unruly streak in them, men who could be tough enough if the occasion warranted, yet men who would balk at shooting another man in the back just because Luke Lilavelt wanted it so.

Added to this was Wall's own reputation. Word of what had happened to Joe Muir would certainly have got around by this time, and have brought hesitation to the more venomous. The minds of men, reflected Wall, ran along unpredictable lines and the power of a known deadly gun carried far. This thought brought a darkness of feeling. Was that to be the sum total of his life? Would men never know him by any other brand? Must what little respect men showed him come from no more worthy attribute than the speed and deadly efficiency of the gun that swung at his hip?

That was the brand that the workings of Luke Lilavelt's scheming had put on him. Oh, there were some few around Basin who, now knowing all the story, would see more to him than the imprint of dark and dangerous years. But to most men the name of Dave Wall would always bring up the grim and shadowy memory.

Like up in the Crimson Hills—up there at Sweet Winds, where Bart Sutton had thanked him for favors done, yet held him at arm's length, remembering not what he was trying to be now, but only what he had been. And what had he been? He had, mused Wall bitterly, never broken his given word, never betrayed any man's confidence. Even in working for Luke Lilavelt he had done his work well. In the running clash of wills between Lilavelt and himself from the very first there had been no deceit on his part. He had despised Lilavelt and told him so and had made answering threat to Lilavelt's threat. When the breaking point came, he'd made no effort to conceal it. Lilavelt knew where he stood.

These things he'd clung to and, though others might never understand them, they brought a certain measure of grim comfort to him. And perhaps not all was lost if a man could respect himself, even where others did not. Rough men he had fought and dominated. Sometimes the weight of his fists had been enough, that and a certain cold and destroying fury that sprang up in him in merciless combat. Again, only his gun could settle the issue, and these were shadows that would follow him all his life. But the stake had been to kill or be killed, and when the issue was that way, it left a man with little choice. And it wasn't done yet, how and where would it end?

The Window Sash spread at Durbin Springs was the most distant one from Basin and it was to this one that Dave Wall rode first. Cash Shelly was the foreman, a lank and bony man, tough enough to handle a tough crew, but the kind, if he were going to throw a gun on you, would tell you so and give you an even break.

Wall reached the layout in the blue twilight of a hot day. Cash Shelly faced him across the littered table in a cabin that passed for the ranch office. A kerosene lamp, badly in need of wick trimming, threw a thin and guttering glow.

"Lilavelt? Not here, Wall," informed Shelly. "A week ago, yes. But not since then. The word was, you're no longer with Window Sash. Right?"

Wall nodded. "What other word did he leave, Cash?"

Shelly considered. Then his eyes flashed and he cut a hand across in front of him with a hard gesture. "I told him to go to hell. It may cost me my job, but I guess I could stand that, too. But what's between him and you is just that, as I see it. If anybody, and that includes you, Wall, was to try and tear this spread apart while I'm foreman, I'd swap lead with him to the last damn' cartridge. But when Lilavelt has a private row on with any one man, that's his personal affair entirely and none of mine."

Wall smiled grimly. "In other words, you refused to dry-gulch me when I wasn't looking?"

"Call it that," conceded Shelly. Then, with the faintest break of humor he added: "You got him scared, man. He's sweating."

"With reason," murmured Wall. "Obliged, Cash."

"There's grub and a bed if you want it," Shelly said. "Lilavelt owes you that much, I think."

"I'll take the grub, but I'll bunk along the trail. I'm riding a Window Sash bronc' that's pretty well done up. How'll you swap for a fresh one?"

"Long as I come out even on my count of saddle stock, I'm satisfied," said Shelly. "You know where the corrals are. Help yourself to what you like."

That night Dave Wall slept close to the earth, a good ten miles along the trail from Durbin Springs. And before he dropped off, he played with the thought that while many men worked for Luke Lilavelt and took his wages, there were few who did not despise him.

Two days later Wall rode up to the headquarters at Pinnacle. It was midmorning. The outfit was off on the range somewhere and the place deserted except for the cook, a one-eyed, profane old pirate called Wind River. Once, for a period of six months, Dave Wall had been foreman of the Pinnacle Ranch. During that time he and Wind River had gotten along very well together. After a period of startled cussing, Wind River said seriously: "Dave, you shouldn't ride in so damn' careless-like. Or maybe you don't know about things?"

"I know," said Wall. "I looked things over pretty careful from back yonder. Lilavelt's been through?"

"Yup. And all of us are supposed to pot-shoot you on sight. Which, of course, don't set worth a damn with some of the boys. But Hub Magley's a surly devil who's got awful big for his britches since Lilavelt made him foreman. I wouldn't trust him far as I can spit. I ain't tryin' to rush you on your way, but . . ."

"Been quite some time since I had a chance at any of your good cooking, Wind River."

Wind River, standing in the door of the cook shack, took a long look around. "Reckon maybe you got time for a bite. You keep watch while I throw a steak in the pan."

When the food was ready, Wind River stood watch at the door while Wall ate. Abruptly the old fellow said: "Damned glad to know you've broke with Lilavelt, Dave. You're too good a man, with too much life ahead of you to waste it workin' for a splinter-legged, crooked side-winder like Luke Lilavelt. Different with me. I'm old and a job's a job. I do my work, mind my own business, and as long as they let it go at that, I'm satisfied. But I'm sure glad you've pulled stakes." Struck with a sudden thought, Wind River turned. "What you after Lilavelt for, Dave?"

Wall grinned. "What makes you think I'm after him?"

"You wouldn't be here if you wasn't," said Wind River bluntly. "And he wouldn't be leavin' orders for you to be smoked down if he didn't know you were after him. Don't fun me, boy. I want to know. Why you after him?"

"For a lot of reasons, Wind River. The main one is that a good man's future and that of his family is at stake. Now you can't tell me some short cut I could take to locate him, could you?"

"I might at that," came Wind River's surprising

retort. "Oh, not direct to him, maybe . . . but a pretty good lead. Lilavelt and Hub Magley had quite a talk together in here at breakfast the morning Lilavelt pulled out. The rest of the crew had finished grubbin' and gone. I was busy washin' up dishes and I guess Lilavelt and Magley didn't figure I could hear what they said, or maybe that it didn't matter if I did. Anyhow, I heard Lilavelt tell Magley that if he wanted to get word to him, not to mail any letters to the regular office in Basin. Instead, Magley was to write direct to some jigger named Dell, at Crater City, and that this feller, Dell, would see that the word got to Lilavelt. Now if that's any good to you, you're welcome."

"Wind River," said Wall, "you're not only the best cook this side the Rockies, you're also a smart old coot and a mighty fine friend. What can I do to make it even with you?"

Wind River considered, then cackled thinly. "Give Lilavelt a damned good boot in the pants for me, once you ketch up with him. God hates a skinflint and so do I. Luke Lilavelt never did stick his long nose into this cook shack that he didn't whine and pule around about how wasteful his ranch cooks were and how the grub bills were breakin' him. And all the time he was lyin' on both counts. Claimin' I ever wasted any grub in all my life is a mortal insult to me. Yeah, you boot him good, boy."

There was an old but comfortable armchair on the porch of the Square S ranch house at Sweet Winds. On this Tracy Sutton spread a blanket, then went inside the house and offered a lithe young shoulder to her father, aiding his slow steps out to the chair, seeing that he was comfortably seated, then spreading another blanket across his knees.

At that moment a rider swung into view past the corrals. Tracy Sutton faced about with a strange, quick eagerness that was not lost upon her father and that put a somber shadow in his eyes. But Tracy's eagerness faded and was replaced with a wistful disappointment.

The rider was Tres Debley and he dismounted and came up to the porch, hat in hand. Bart Sutton stared, then growled: "You're Debley, of course. Remember you now. What can I do for you?"

"Just came to pay my respects," said Tres quietly. "That and to ask if Dave Wall has happened to drop by lately? I was hoping to meet him somewhere up in this country."

Tres Debley was a little surprised to see how gaunt and old and tired Bart Sutton looked. He'd thought that the cattleman would have completely recovered by this time from the wounded side he'd collected from the gun of Nick Karnes. Sutton seemed to read the thought.

"It was a wise man who first said that there was no fool like an old one," he rumbled. "I wouldn't listen to Tracy. I would try and get around again before I should have. So I tore things loose again and went back to bed for a real spell. I'm a damned nuisance and plumb fed up with myself. What makes you think that Wall is back in this part of the country again?"

"He's on a trail that could have led him up here." Tres felt the girl's glance upon him and, meeting it, was startled at how she seemed to be hanging on his every word.

"What kind of a trail?" asked Sutton.

The look on Tracy Sutton's face gave Tres sudden inspiration. He settled down on the top step of the porch, laid his hat beside him, and built a cigarette.

"Dave is trying to run down Luke Lilavelt. For the best of reasons. If you'd care to listen, I'll tell you the whole story. Don't know whether Dave would thank me for telling it, but in justice to him I think it might help if you heard it."

Tres glanced at Tracy Sutton again, and she said, with almost breathless swiftness: "Please."

It was Bart Sutton's turn to throw a glance at his daughter. He sighed deeply and growled: "Go ahead. We're listening."

So Tres told it as he knew it, told it all. When he finished, he flashed another look at Tracy Sutton. She wasn't watching him, but, instead, was staring out across the sweep of open country that fell away to the distant desert. Her eyes were misty, and if Tres Debley had ever glimpsed a soft and glowing glory on a human face, he saw it now. Tres cleared his throat and ended, a little gruffly, "So you see, Mister Sutton, rather than being what a lot of people thought he was, Dave Wall is really one of the biggest men who ever walked. He set out to do a tough job in the only way it could be done, as he saw it. He knew the price he'd have to pay, but he was more than willing to pay it. Yeah, I want somebody to show me a bigger man than Dave Wall."

Bart Sutton was silent for some little time. "It adds up," he said finally. "It explains a lot of things. Things I've done plenty of wondering about. Somehow I felt all along that the man was a double personality, but I couldn't figure why he was. I agree with you, Debley. Only a big man could have done what he did . . . a damned big man. I'm glad you've told Tracy and me. It . . . helps."

Sutton looked at Tracy again, with great fondness and an abrupt shedding of the shadowed somberness that he had shown previously. Tracy, stirring at last, went to the door. "You'll stay and have dinner with Dad and me, Mister Debley?"

"It would be a privilege, ma'am," said Tres.

It was a good meal and before it was done it

seemed to Tres Debley that Bart Sutton looked ten years younger. Sutton told Tres that as far as he knew, Luke Lilavelt was nowhere in the vicinity. "We haven't had a lick of trouble with Window Sash since that affair below the Monuments, when you and Wall turned that herd back. Yeah, I heard all about that. Something else I owe you and Wall for. As for Lilavelt, if any word of him was loose around here, my riders would pick it up and bring it to me."

"Maybe Dave has already caught up with him somewhere along the trail," said Tres. "If he has, he'll drop me a letter to that effect."

Tres didn't bring up his own reason for being in the Crimson Hills country. That was between him and Hippo Dell. He'd look to other and far more likely spots than this fine ranch for the trail of Hippo Dell.

When Tres went out to leave, after thanking Tracy and her father for their hospitality, Tracy followed him to where his horse stood, hip-shot and drowsing. Tracy seemed shy, hesitant, a little at a loss for words.

"When . . . when you see Dave . . . Mister Wall again, you'll tell him not to forget that he has friends at Sweet Winds?"

Tres smiled at her. "I wouldn't worry about that, Miss Sutton. I doubt very much that Dave Wall has forgotten for a single minute this ranch of Sweet Winds . . . and the people who live here. Particularly the people. Particularly one person. Me . . . I don't see how he could."

She colored hotly, but her eyes did not waver, and he left her that way, watching him as he rode off. Tres wisely knew that beyond him, she was seeing Dave Wall.

Tres rode into Crater City at midafternoon. In the general store, which was also the post office, he asked if there was any mail for him, found there wasn't, so went out again, pausing in the shade of the overhang to build a smoke. In him was stirring the restlessness of a man who had set out on a purpose he'd felt was important and had then, along the way, come to realize that it wasn't nearly as important as he thought. For the beating Tres had taken at the hands of Hippo Dell had become considerably distant now, and the first great anger and wish for retribution had oddly burned out. There was not a single bruise or sore spot left to remind him, and he thought that it would probably take actual sight of Dell, to get him stirred up again. Even that might not make him react. A man absorbed a licking, got over it and, given time, forgot it, providing the memory of it was not rubbed in too strongly.

Practically speaking, Tres realized now that he hadn't been too smart in leaving Basin and making this long ride up here. True, he might cut Dave Wall's trail, but that chance could be days or weeks away. Maybe by this time Luke Lilavelt had been taken by Dave back to Basin for questioning by Judge Masterson. Maybe out of those questions some line on Big George Yearly had been gotten, in which case Dave might be traveling far, very far indeed, to try and collect Yearly.

About the only thing, Tres reflected, that had made this trip to the Crimson Hills worthwhile was the chance he'd had to set the Suttons right about Dave Wall's real make-up. The look on Tracy Sutton's face had been full payment for that!

Tres left the store porch and headed for The Rialto, remembering the shoot-out that had taken place there that had come so close to claiming Bart Sutton's life. Quite a lot of things had taken place since that day.

From the mouth of an alley, gray with afternoon shadow, a voice reached him, mildly humorous.

"Some people are always underfoot."

Tres jerked, stared, then ducked into the alley. "Dave! I'll be damned! How long you been here?"

"Stretch the time and make it ten minutes," drawled Wall. "Just arrived, in fact."

"What's the idea, skulking in this hole?"

"Starting a watch. May be a damned long one. But for better or worse I'm going to make it."

"A watch for what?" demanded Tres.

"Not for what . . . for whom," drawled Wall. "Friend of yours. Hippo Dell." Tres looked a little bewildered. Wall showed a small grin, dropped his hand on Tres's arm. "Hunker down and take it easy. I'll tell you all about it."

Wall suited his action to the words, dropping on his heels, the long curve of his dusty shirt back against a handy wall. Tres squatted beside him and said: "You look like a wolf that's been run steady for a week. I thought the man you were after was Luke Lilavelt?"

"Is," stated Wall laconically. "But I've got to find Hippo Dell before I can find Lilavelt. It's like this." And then Wall told of what he'd learned from Wind River, the old cook at the Window Sash spread at Pinnacle. "It shapes up that Lilavelt feels sure I'm on his trail, but not for the reason I really am. He's left word at all his spreads that I'm to be diced quick and final if I show at any of them. The big hole in that is that he doesn't realize that all men are not as low-down and crooked as he is. Anyhow, he's hoping I'll get rocked off and Hub Magley, ramrod at Pinnacle, is to get word to him as soon as I am, so that Lilavelt can break out of wherever he's hiding and get back to the affairs of living again."

"And Hippo Dell is the one to relay the word from Magley to Lilavelt?" said Tres.

"That's it. Oh, friend Luke is a fine, brave specimen, all right. Not going to drop into any town to ask for his mail direct. He's playing everything close to his vest, Luke is." Wall spat in disgust.

"Might be a week before Dell shows up here," said Tres.

Wall nodded. "That's right, it might be. And that worries me some, for I don't know how long Judge Masterson can hold off extradition on Jerry Connell. Then again, Hippo might show up ten minutes from now. Either way, it's the only straight lead I've been able to pick up so I've got to ride with it. Only one thing . . ." Wall paused, frowning.

"What's that?" Tres asked.

"There's a chance that Lilavelt may be hiding out somewhere around the Crimson Hills head-quarters. Seems like he's been more or less working up this way. I'd like to ride a prowl up that way and have a look at things. Yet if I drew a blank there and Dell came in to town while I was gone . . ."

"We'll fix that, easy," declared Tres. "You look like you could stand being away from a saddle for a little while. You stay put right here, and I'll do the prowling around Crimson Hills. I know that country better than you do, anyhow. I can be out there by sundown and dark's a good time to prowl."

"That would help a heap, cowboy," Wall admitted. "Only, should you get a look at Hippo Dell, don't you go trying to throw a loop on him. He's the one to lead me to Lilavelt. Your chore with Dell can wait until later."

Tres stood up. "I'm a patient man. I'll be back here sometime tonight."

"I'll be looking for you," promised Wall. "Remember, you're to see, but not be seen."

The chuff of Tres's spurs died away in the dust of the street, and then, too, faintly the departing clump of his horse. Dave Wall settled a little more deeply on his heels, sagged more fully against the wall at his back. There was a deeper weariness in him than he had thought. It lay across his shoulders and down his saddle-leaned flanks in a steady ache. Tough and hardy as he was, he had driven himself remorselessly over the past several days, and too much riding and not enough sleep had piled up its inevitable total. But he couldn't stop, couldn't rest. Pounding all the time at the back of his brain was the realization that time was vital. Judge Masterson would get all that he could for Jerry, but the judge himself had admitted a limit to what he could do. Maybe a month, the judge had said. After that, well, once John Ogden got Jerry back to Round Mountain . . .

Wall shook himself, driving the thought from his mind. He'd get Lilavelt and Lilavelt would talk if he had to burn it out of him. And even if what Lilavelt had to say did not lead immediately to Big George Yearly, just knowledge that Yearly was alive and able to be located was bound to help Jerry's case. It might be grounds that would enable Judge Masterson to win further delay of some kind.

That was the way Wall's thoughts ran, but in a little while they grew sluggish and faded out altogether, and before he realized it he had slipped off into an uneasy doze; his head dropped on his chest, his shoulders falling slack and loose. Without the support at his back, he would have toppled over. The sun dipped lower, shadows lengthened and deepened. A blue gloom filled the alley and Wall was only a part of the motionless shadow there.

He awakened suddenly, yet with dulled senses. It came down through the blur of his mind that he'd heard a horse go by along the street. The significance of this dragged heavily across his fatigue-drugged mind, then sharpened into sudden focus. He came erect suddenly and the protest of his stiffened muscles was a knife edge of pure pain that wrung a muffled curse from him. He steadied himself, then limped to the corner of the building at his left and peered carefully along the sunset street.

A saddle mount was at the hitch rail before the general store, so recently left that it was still restless, not yet settled down. Well, what did that mean? Just a saddle horse that could have been ridden into town by any one of a hundred persons. But it might have borne the man he was looking for—Hippo Dell.

A wry and mirthless smile pulled at Wall's lips. That would be asking too much of luck or the smiles of a fortune which so far had not been overly kind toward him. Yet, from now on any horse or any rider that entered this town of Crater City had to be watched and reckoned with. As he had told Tres Debley, what Wind River had told him was the only lead he had so far been able to pick up and he had to ride with it, gambling that the old cook had heard right and told him the same. Wall tumbled a sack of tobacco from his shirt pocket, rolled a smoke, lipped it, and searched the band of his hat for a match. But he did not strike it.

Movement on the store porch, movement in the blue shadow there. The bulk of a man. A heavy man, a fat brute of a man. Hippo Dell. Coming down off the porch in that ponderous but queerly light way of his, carrying a sack of provisions in one fist. He put the sack across the pommel of his saddle, swung up, and came riding back up the street.

Dave Wall flattened back against the side of the alley. His first impulse was to step out, throw a gun on Dell, with the half-formed thought of thus forcing Dell to lead him to Luke Lilavelt. But instantly he knew that this would not do. He had seen enough of Hippo Dell to know that here was a man with unguessed depths of toughness in him, a man you might trail, but never force. There was only one way—the slower, more cautious one.

Hippo Dell rode on past the alley mouth, as light in his saddle for a big man as he was on his feet. He went straight through town and out into the open country beyond. Once sure of this, Wall went back through the alley with long strides, to where he had left his horse beside an old freight corral out back. He tightened the girth he had loosened, swung up, and cut around the fringe of town, past some old shanties and tin-can littered flats.

Through the false glow of sunset he picked up Hippo Dell's bobbing figure breaking well down into the open country, on a line that would take him somewhere near the Stinking Water–Monument gap. Realization struck Wall that it wasn't going to be easy to follow that trail. In less than an hour it would be dark, and that was a wide, wide, country Dell was heading into. And the man was just sly and foxy enough to set one trail direction, then swing to another, once it was fully dark. No, it wouldn't be easy. But it had to be tried. It still wasn't dark enough to start following directly. If he could see Dell, then by a backward glance Dell could see him. He would, Wall realized, go faster by going more slowly. Here was a place where he had to use his head. So he sat his still horse and watched, watched until Hippo Dell vanished into the clotting dusk, leaving only two things to mark his way—a direction that did not deviate at all, and the tracks his horse left on the slowly cooling earth.

Wall turned then and rode back into town. At the livery barn he ordered his horse a full feed of oats and hay and a rub-down. For himself, he went into Charlie Ring's hash house and took on a full meal, eating slowly and making the most of the chance to rest. Before he finished, he had Charlie make him up a couple of thick steak sandwiches and put them in a small sugar sack. And then as he paid and got ready to leave, he said: "Tres Debley will probably drop in here later tonight, Charlie. Tell him the man came to get the mail and that I'm on my way. Tell him I'll see him in Basin. And tell nobody else I said anything."

Charlie nodded and said shrewdly: "Hope you find what you're after, Wall."

Chapter Ten

Miles out from Crater City, Dave Wall watched the moon come up. This he had counted on. He knew what the full moon was like on a still, warm night out in the open country and across the desert, so bright and full-glowing it threw definite shadows. To this trail he was bringing the full concentration of knowledge and experience and observation. Men, he knew, unless trying to throw a false trail, traveled from one place to another by as straight a line as natural obstacles would allow. And the more he thought of it, the stronger the conclusion that Hippo Dell was not out to throw a false trail. The man, apparently, had felt that no one was concerned in his business in the slightest way. The confident manner in which he had ridden into and out of Crater City proved that. Hippo Dell had been around the Crimson Hills country for some time. He had been in Crater City on many occasions, no doubt. His coming and going would mean nothing to the people there. Night, distance, the desert—these things would cover up all that Hippo Dell had to hide. So, decided Wall, would Dell reason.

With the true line of Dell's departure fixed solidly in his mind, Dave Wall had already stopped several times before the moon showed and, leaning close to the earth on foot, had, by flickering match light, quartered back and forth until he had found what he looked for. Fresh hoof marks. Now, while the moon climbed and laid its full effulgence across the world, he again discerned the trace and could go steadily ahead.

In several places, after moving away from the harder upland earth, he struck stretches of red sand where he was able to move his horse ahead at a jog, for cut deep against the moon's smooth earth reflection, the hoof gouges of the horse ahead loomed plain.

He saw the Monuments rise spectrally off to his right and drift behind him. The trail crossed above the Stinking Water swamps, drove straight on into the desert. The going was better than he hoped. He had, at the start, figured on a fairly good lead for a part of the night, then a few hours of sleep and a fresh attack on the trail in the morning. But at this rate, there seemed a fair chance that he might come up with Hippo Dell's objective before the night was done. This, thought Wall grimly, he would prefer, for the night would offer an element of surprise attack that daylight would not.

He had no idea what sort of hide-out Luke Lilavelt would have, here in the desert. Hardly a comfortable one, at best. Just a frugal, dismal camp in some dry wash probably, where an isolated pool of brackish water made life possible for man or animal. And it was reasonable to believe that it would not be too distant from Crater City, for the desert was the desert, and a man, with any luck at all, could do as good a job of hiding ten or fifteen miles into it as he could a hundred. But no part of it was ever pleasant enough to call a man into it unless by necessity. There were plenty of areas in it that did not see a single rider once a year.

Wall got a grim satisfaction in the thought of Luke Lilavelt's seeking its harsh sanctuary through fear of the man he had once pushed and ordered around in mean and dominating arrogance. He had been sure of his power over that man and taking advantage of it. He imagined Luke Lilavelt, whose way it was to complain even in comfortable circumstances, sleeping on the ground and finding only discomfort there, while other men, inured to it, found rest. Lilavelt, following some thin line of shade around a sage or greasewood clump, or against some sun-scorched cutbank, would have sought a comfort and coolness that simply wasn't there, eating rough and frugal and monotonous food under rough conditions.

These were things that bigger-souled men knew how to accept without complaint, buttressed by the stoicism of their strength and courage. But Luke Lilavelt didn't have that courage. The brackish water would scour his throat and rest uneasily in a queasy stomach. The sun would burn and ache in his eyes and Lilavelt would curse it and find no ease anywhere. And all of this he would endure because of fear—fear of one man. Of Dave Wall. It was something to find a raw and macabre pleasure in.

Wall struck the first wide stretches of stunted sage and clumps of greasewood. He stopped at the edge of this, located those hoof marks once more, fixed their direction, and went ahead. This was a chance he had to take. The trail would go through and somewhere beyond hit an open stretch where he could locate it again.

For a full mile he rode the scanty but persistent brush, and here the moon seemed less bright, for the cover drew in the light and did not reflect it back. Abruptly a furrow of shadow lay at right angles across the way. Wall's horse stopped of its own accord, tossing its head. Here ran one of the numerous washes that cut and gouged the desert, starting nowhere in particular, then meandering on perhaps for miles before frittering out with the same lack of plan with which they started.

Wall sat his horse for a long time, all senses sharp and reaching as he keened the night. The world was utterly still, except for the faintest brush of air, drifting from south to north. Wall dismounted, let himself down over the edge of the wash, and prowled a distance up and down, moving with the greatest care, using the tricky light to locate places where the north bank of the wash was sloped or caved down enough to permit easy entrance by a horse.

He took off his hat and scratched matches and shielded them in the tall crown, using these brief flickers of truer light to study these spots. He found four before he came to another that showed the fresh-cut, gouging slashes of descending hoofs. He went directly across the wash from this spot and began looking for places there where a horse had climbed out. But though there were a number of such likely spots, none showed the betraying hoof marks. Instead, nearly a hundred yards east of where the trail led into the wash, he found tracks following the bottom of the wash itself.

He went back to his horse, increasing eagerness in his stride. He fell back a good seventy-five yards from the wash and then rode slowly, paralleling its north bank. A thin and coiling tension ran up and down his spine. The end of this trail wasn't very far away. Instinctively he knew that, was as sure of it as he had ever been of anything. Water holes in the desert were always in washes and the trail had led definitely into this one. Somewhere out there was the camp— and the man.

That lazy push of air from the south was a tricky and wayward thing. Sometimes it was steady, then it would come in little puffs, and again it would die out altogether. When this happened, Wall would rein in and wait for it to come on again. For he needed that drift of air. On it would come evidence of the camp.

He rode so far he thought he must have missed it and was considering retracing his route. And then he got it. It came abruptly and sure, on one of those wayward puffs of air. The acrid odor of a dying campfire, part smoke, part the bite of charred wood. There might have been something else, or perhaps that was just a touch of an overly stimulated imagination. But it seemed to Wall that he could pick up the tang of tobacco smoke.

He was out of his saddle swiftly, ground-reining his horse. From the scabbard under the stirrup leather he dragged his Winchester rifle. He took off his spurs and hung them on his saddle horn. Then, crouched low, he went in, making sure of every step before he put his weight down. The odors of the camp grew stronger as he drew closer to the wash. The final twenty yards he made on hands and knees, placing his rifle carefully before him with each movement. The last ten feet he was snake-flat on his stomach, his hat discarded, until he was able to inch his eyes over the crest of the bank.

This cutbank was fairly high, eight or ten feet, and it was fairly dark beneath, dark except for a thin scatter of dying coals. But men were down there, two of them, smoking. So abruptly that it was as startling as a gunshot would have been, the voice of Luke Lilavelt came up to Wall, droning and nasal and tight with a rasping, complaining anger.

"You sure there wasn't any letter for you in Crater City, George? Hub Magley promised. . . ."

"Hell with Magley," cut in Hippo Dell's voice, moist but slurred with anger. "Hell with you, too, in a minute. I've told you a dozen times there wasn't any mail. And I've told you that many times not to call me by that name. I'm Hippo Dell, understand . . . Hippo Dell! Nothing else."

"I keep forgetting," mumbled Lilavelt sulkily. "If I lay out in this damned desert much longer, I'll forget my own name. You needn't get so proddy about it. The way you act you'd think forty sheriffs were listening in."

"That's not the point. The name George Yearly don't exist any more. It's done with . . . forgotten. If you and me were in a small boat alone in the middle of the ocean, you couldn't call me George Yearly. I'd be Hippo Dell there, just like I am here. Now don't you forget again or I'll slap you butter-legged and leave you here to starve. And you'd do that, too . . . rather than go out and take your chances with Wall." The words ended with a snap of vast contempt.

Dave Wall lay like a log, scarce daring to

breathe. A name was rocketing through his head. George Yearly. Big George Yearly. It was the answer to so many things . . . the answer to everything. He was down there . . . not twenty feet away. Hippo Dell . . . but not Hippo Dell. Big George Yearly . . . It added up. It added up so perfectly that he wondered why he hadn't guessed it before. The angle that Cole Ashabaugh had brought forth in Judge Masterson's office back at Basin—how true it had been.

Luke Lilavelt was speaking again. "Maybe that letter from Hub Magley will show up tomorrow. Somewhere along the line some of my boys are sure to catch up with Wall. He can't be as lucky all the time as he was at Gravelly. Cube Spayd and Joe Muir sure botched that deal. And they had Wall dead to rights. Well, they're both dead now, and they ought to be . . . after that." There was a heartless venom in Lilavelt's words.

Hippo Dell said: "You're a pretty mean specimen, Lilavelt, about as mean as they come. A lot of thanks any man gets for laying his life on the line for you. You might as well understand one thing right now. It's your money I love . . . not you. And forget this damned caterwauling about luck. It ain't luck with Dave Wall. I've told you that before. I don't like that man any better than you do, but I'm well aware of one thing. He's a tough *hombre* and he's no fool. After that deal at Gravelly, do you think he's going to walk into a set-up like that at any other of your spreads? Maybe you do, but I don't. The reason we haven't heard from Magley is because he's had no word to send. Maybe he never will. If you had an ounce of guts, you'd head on out and take your chances with Wall."

"Maybe I will," muttered Lilavelt. "Maybe I will."

Hippo Dell laughed scoffingly. "That's something else you've said a hundred times. I don't believe it."

"You should talk!" shrilled Lilavelt in sudden mean anger. "How long have you been on the dodge? I don't see you going back to Round Mountain and . . ."

"Shut up! Shut up, damn you . . . or I'll throw a slug into you right here and now! Shut up!"

Dave Wall held his breath, waiting for the snarl of a gun, for its lancing tongue of crimson venom. For in Hippo Dell's voice had been a wild, killing note. But the silence settled in and held for a long time. Then came apology from Lilavelt, which in its whining servility was more contemptible than his other meanness had been.

"All right, Hippo . . . I take it back. You and me, we can't afford to row. There's too much money ahead for both of us to start calling names and arguing over nothing. It's tough waiting, all around. But things will straighten out."

"Shut up," rapped Hippo again. But this time that wild, killing note was gone.

Silent as a shadow, Dave Wall inched back from the rim of the wash until he had a couple of yards of leeway. Then he lay, thinking things out. Luke Lilavelt, he realized didn't count at all any more. But Hippo Dell—Big George Yearly— did. He had to get Hippo Dell to Basin, and get him there alive. But how to do it?

Throwing a gun on the man wouldn't be enough. The man was smart, he was desperate and a fighter. Even with a gun leveled at him he'd take his chance and go for his own. Besides, in the tricky night light, anything could happen in gun work.

As far as Wall could see, there was only one way. Let the camp quiet down, get deep in sleep. Then circle a bit, drop into the wash, and sneak up on the camp. Locate the sleeping Dell and cool him with a gun barrel—pistol-whip him. Then tie him up before consciousness returned.

This had its risks, too. There was always the chance of discovery, of alarm. Dell and Lilavelt had horses somewhere, either up or down the wash from the camp. A snort from one of them, even an uneasy stirring could do the trick. But these were chances that had to be taken, for there was no other solution.

It was characteristic of Dave Wall that once he had cast up all the possibilities, he made his decision without further hesitation and then set about figuring out all his moves. First things first. Where were those horses?

Wall pushed himself up to a kneeling position and strained his ears against the noiseless pulsing of the night. Below the wash rim a few low murmured words passed back and forth, but these weren't what Wall was interested in just now. He listened until there was a roaring in his ears and he dropped his mouth open to ease the pressure. At long last he got it, faint but definite. Down the wash it was, to his left, the stirring of weary hoofs on hard-packed gravel.

Wall dropped down, prone again, letting the tension run out of him. So much for that. The horses were below the camp, so it would be his move to come in from above. But not yet—not for a long time.

He rolled over on his back, face to the white moonlight. He knew a swift hunger for a cigarette, but put this thought aside instantly. His mind went back across the past several days, recalling the long and empty miles he had ridden in his search for Luke Lilavelt. A blank trail, promising nothing until an old, one-eyed ranch cook who had listened and remembered, and who valued an old friendship, had given him a lead to follow.

So now the trail's end was here, out in this lonely desert country. Within short yards of him was Luke Lilavelt. But of so much greater importance, so was Hippo Dell—and Dell was the one he wanted. Wall marked the slow sweep of the moon and waited it out.

He was chill and stiff as he started his stalk on the camp. He worked back up the wash for a good fifty yards before lowering himself carefully down a shelving break. He had left his rifle behind, for it would be of no aid to him at all in this sort of affair. This would be close, fast work and Wall knew the grim hope that it would be fast enough.

He went down the wash with a tensing caution that was more exhausting than hard physical effort would have been. Here in this depression the light was vastly tricky, for there were smears and lines of moon glow, but there were also figures of dark shadow, close to the banks of the wash and this varied as the height of the banks varied.

To his probing eyes the moonlight seemed to take on the quality of fluid, to flow and coil and shift. This, Wall knew, was purely illusory, but it was an illusion that persisted. Every cautious step was an effort full of strain, for it had to be a noiseless one, the toe touching first, testing what was underneath before full weight could be put upon the foot. The all-over strain settled in the pit of Wall's stomach, tying it up in a knot.

But he was there at last. On the alkali-whitened gravel of the wash, the area where the fire had burned was a dark smear. Small bulking piles of equipment lay about. And the men—the two men.

Motionless, Wall reconstructed things. Lying up there on the rim of the wash, Lilavelt's voice had been a little to the right and that of Dell to the left. It was reasonable to figure they had been lounging on their respective bedrolls. And that would be how they were sleeping now, Lilavelt the nearer to him, Dell that bulk yonder, half in the glow of the moon, half shrouded by the shadow cast by the wash rim.

It would have been supremely easy to have handled Luke Lilavelt first. Two long, swift strides, the slash of a gun barrel, and Lilavelt would be taken care of. But that would have meant a certain degree of sound, and who could tell how Hippo Dell would react? Remembering the man and his sly, soft ways, his deceptively light movement despite his bulk, it had always seemed to Wall that there was something feline about him. And maybe he slept like a cat, just as lightly and unpredictably.

So it had to be Dell first. It didn't matter if Lilavelt woke after that. Wall had little fear, and only a vast contempt for Luke Lilavelt's physical prowess. He started on toward Hippo Dell.

For the past weeks, Luke Lilavelt's periods of sleep had been fitful and uneasy. In his first black, blind anger on hearing from the lips of Joe

Muir what had happened up at the Crimson Hills spread when Dave Wall had first arrived there to take over, of the firing of Nick Karnes and Whitey Brewer, and later, of the killing of them, Lilavelt had gone straight to Judge Masterson in Basin and opened the case against Jerry Connell's past. This was what he had threatened to do if Wall ever turned against Window Sash interests, and this was what he had done.

Yet, only minutes after the fact, when cooler reason had begun to replace blind anger, the realization hit Lilavelt that in making this move he had lost his hold on Dave Wall, and that he had turned loose the forces of retribution. He recalled the threats he had made and the answering threats Wall had given him. And he knew that Wall would try and make good.

That was when the great fear had started to gnaw at him, and it was something that had remained and grown until it rode his shoulder endlessly. His plans and schemes to have Wall removed permanently from the picture hadn't worked out and that fact didn't lighten the load of fear in any way. And so the haunting cloud had grown heavier and darker with every passing day until Lilavelt couldn't get rid of it even when he slept. More than one night since then he had awakened, sweating and shivering at the same time, hag-ridden by his own fears.

He awoke now, opening his eyes to the white

beat of moonlight. He blinked, recalling where he was, then knowing a cooling rush of reassurance through the night's vast stillness. He stirred a little under his blanket, took another look around, went still and stricken.

Was he seeing things? That out there—was it the tall figure of a man, or just an illusion of disordered fancy? Panic rose in Lilavelt, caught him by the throat. He fumbled under his blanket for the gun he kept there constantly.

No—it wasn't fancy—it was real. That figure out there . . . Lilavelt's throat unlocked and fear shrilled out. "George . . . George . . . !"

He pushed out with his gun, pulled the trigger. There was jumbled fear in that move, too, for the weapon was not clear of his blanket. So the lead flew wide, but the bellow of report was a thunderclap in the night. Lilavelt clawed the weapon free of the muffling blanket, fired again and again, blindly, frantically.

And then, from where that shadow figure loomed came the pale lash of answering gun flame. A stunning blow hammered Luke Lilavelt in the center of his scrawny chest. It brought with it a crushing force and one thin, deep drag of agony. And these let in a flood of everlasting blackness.

Dave Wall had heard that first stir of Lilavelt's. It had brought him half around, gun drawn, his breath locked and held. Men stirred in their sleep—this could mean nothing. But it proved to mean everything. For there had come Lilavelt's fear-driven cry of discovery and after that the hammering bellow of a gun. Clear and raw, realization came to Dave Wall what he had to do. The issue was forced now. So far none of Lilavelt's shots had come close. But there could always be another—and there was still Hippo Dell. Wall drove a single shot into the center of the rearing bulk that was Luke Lilavelt, then whirled and drove for that far more dangerous and valuable bulk that was Hippo Dell.

Hippo was half clear of his blankets and chopping down with his gun when Dave Wall crashed down upon him. Hippo's right arm, coming down, was met just short of the elbow by Wall's driving shoulder. The gun roared uselessly and the leverage of impact spun the weapon out of his hand.

Wall had no better luck. He swung his weapon savagely at Hippo's head, but his initial dive had been a little long and the gun struck past Hippo's head, crashed on the unyielding gravel beyond. And then Hippo's bunched knees, driving up, tossed Wall completely clear and face foremost into that same gravel. Wall turned completely over, right arm doubled under him, wrenched so savagely that it went numb.

Wall came struggling up, knowing two things.

He'd lost his gun and he had the fight of his life on his hands. It came swiftly but clearly to him, the things Tom Burke and Tres Debley had told him about this man, Hippo Dell. Strong— strong—and cat-fast. Wall lunged in at a man just rising from his knees. Wall's left fist, curving up, skidded off the side of Hippo's beefy face. Then one of Hippo's fists crashed into the middle of Wall's body. It was like a ponderous club, it hurt him all through, seemed to drain him of all breath.

Wall staggered back, marveling that his feet were under him. But this was jungle warfare, no rules, no mercy. Wall kicked at Hippo, felt his boot sink into Hippo's gross torso. It brought Hippo forward, bent over. Wall clamped his left arm around Hippo's neck, hung on desperately. It was like trying to cling to a grizzly bear. Hippo had his feet fully under him now and he lurched back and forth, whipping Wall about like he was worrying a sack. His ponderous fists beat and pounded and all that saved Wall at the moment was that he clung too close for Hippo to get full, driving length to the blows.

The numbness was leaving Wall's right arm now, so he brought his hand up, drove the heel of it under Hippo's chin, and put all he had into a savage upward lift. He could feel Hippo fighting back, all the power of his thick neck bent to the effort. But the leverage was in Wall's favor here and inch by inch he drove Hippo's head up and back. There was a critical point in this, and when it was reached, Hippo's head snapped all the way back and he loosed all hold on Wall and tried to lunge clear.

But it had come to Wall what he had to do, his only chance to win this affair. And he acted now on the knowledge. His right hand slid down under Hippo's chin and his fingers dug into Hippo's throat. He snapped his left hand in to join the right. Then he sat down. It was big and round, that throat, with a surface layer that was soft, but with thick muscles inside. Wall's digging fingers became the focal point of all the strength and energy he possessed. And now came some savage moments that were pure nightmare. For a little time Hippo beat at Wall like some insensate animal, but Wall had his head jammed tight against Hippo's chest, his shoulders hunched to protect the angles of his jaw, so Hippo's clubbing fists had little to hammer at except Wall's arched back. Even so the blows shook Wall all through and made him realize that his only chance was to keep his grip on Hippo's throat.

Abruptly Hippo left off trying to club Wall off him. He locked his arms about Wall's body and clamped down. Here, Wall realized, was that tremendous strength that Tom Burke and Tres Debley had warned about. It was as though bands of steel had suddenly wound around him, drawing tighter and tighter with a power calculated to crush and rend everything.

Wall called on the sinew and rawhide in his tempered body to fight off that ghastly pressure. For he could feel his ribs spring and his spine start taking on a slow numbness. His heart pounded wildly, like a thing caged and his breath piled up in his throat. But his fingers stayed in Hippo's throat and gradually sank deeper, biting through the protecting muscles, cutting off the big man's wind. But a deep and deadly agony was building up in Wall and he wondered, a little dimly, how long he could stand this.

Without warning, Hippo fell sideways to the hard gravel and whitened cobbles of the dry wash bed, carrying Wall with him. And then Hippo started rolling over and over, throwing his ponderous weight on Wall with each turn. What punishment Wall took was brutal. Cobbles ground and dug at the back of his head, at his shoulders. Hippo let go his grinding grip, rolled faster and faster, arms and legs beginning to thrash wildly. Yet that grip on his throat was doing its deadly work. His fight for air became a thin, agonized whistling.

Over and over—back and forth—they rolled through the spot where the fire had been. They rolled over a tin coffee pot, crushed it flat. And each time Hippo's wild bulk rolled over him, Wall thought he was done for. There was a vast roaring in Wall's ears, the taste of blood in his mouth and throat. Hippo quit rolling. They lay on their sides. Gathering a final gust of strength he marveled at possessing, Wall swung himself on top of his man. Now, with a betraying wildness, Hippo began clawing at Wall's arms, trying to tear that deadly grip from his throat. Wall fought back, hanging on—hanging on, breath sobbing through set teeth.

Hippo's gross torso began to arc up and up, like some spring under dreadful torment, taut with a terrible, shaking intensity. His efforts for breath was a horror to which Dave Wall was insensate. And then, like something that had broken all the way through, Hippo Dell went completely still and flaccid.

Feeling all the resistance run out of his man, Dave Wall relaxed his grip, lurched to his feet. He immediately fell down again, for all the world was reeling and crazy. He got up and fell down twice more before, on another try, he managed to hold his feet. Then he stumbled about, only dimly understanding what he was searching for.

He found them presently, piled to one side. Saddles, with coiled ropes strapped to them. Only some deep and driving instinct kept Wall at it. He tipped Hippo Dell on his side, pulled his limp arms behind him, looped rope around them, and drew them savagely tight. He tied

Hippo's ankles together, pulled them up and back as far as he could, and so, with a short length of rope between them and Hippo's wrists, had his man helpless.

Then Wall flattened fully out, his head on his folded arms, and fought back the nausea and weary sickness that tried to engulf him. He felt the savage pounding of his heart, the deep hunger in his aching lungs for air, would never cease. But it did, gradually, and the wicked pulse behind his eyes slowly stilled.

He was weary and beaten when he finally straightened up, and he marveled that a man could exhaust so much of himself and still live. How about Hippo Dell? Had he held onto Hippo's throat too long?

The thought brought a sudden start of worry. For Hippo dead would mean nothing, but Hippo alive meant Big George Yearly. He leaned over the man and knew a swift rush of relief. Hippo was breathing, roughly and hurriedly. It was like quickening drops of water, building to a fullness of a steady flow.

Wall went over to where another man lay. He scratched a match and had a look, sure of what he would find even before the faint light bloomed. Luke Lilavelt was as unlovely in death as he had been in life. The match went out and Wall straightened, staring away over the still and lonely night.

He knew no triumph over this particular feat. How long ago had it been since he'd promised such an ending for Luke Lilavelt—promised it directly to Lilavelt himself? Well, it didn't matter now. When it came, it had been a thing of desperate necessity, rather than choice. What would Cole Ashabaugh and Judge Masterson have to say about it? Would they believe him? He pushed a weary hand across his face and quit trying to think.

Chapter Eleven

Driving a buckboard that he'd hired at the livery barn in Basin, John Ogden came up to the Connell Ranch on Magpie Creek. The afternoon was well along and the little ranch layout seemed to drowse contentedly against a background of its own forming shadows.

Judith Connell, a slender figure in gingham, was puttering among the flowers in the little garden along the south side of the ranch house. The twins were playing beside her and in a homemade cradle, standing just at the borderline of sunlight and shadow, their baby sister slept peacefully under a canopy of mosquito netting.

Brushing back a wayward lock of hair, Judith turned at the sound of the buckboard's approach. She looked very girlish as she stood there with the slanting sunlight warming her face and throat and shining on her bared head. She wondered who this tall, grizzled, stern-faced man might be. She moved out to meet him, the twins plucking at her skirt, big-eyed and curious.

John Ogden stepped from the buckboard, took off his hat. "You," he asked quietly, "are Missus Connell . . . Missus Jerry Connell?"

"Yes." A flicker of alarm showed in Judith's

eyes. "Jerry . . . he's all right? Nothing has happened . . . ?"

"No," said Ogden gently. "Nothing has happened to Jerry. But I think it has to me." He paused, looking at the twins with a strange, quick yearning in his deep eyes. "I find myself a man without direction or purpose and I think . . . no, I know I'm glad."

Judith was puzzled. She had a trick of crinkling her nose slightly when she frowned. "I don't understand, Mister . . . ?"

"Ogden. John Ogden."

Judith gave back a step. She'd heard about this man—heard plenty. She grew very straight and her eyes grew hard with an accusing light. "So you are . . . John Ogden. The man who wants to . . . to hang my husband. You . . ."

John Ogden winced slightly, spun his hat in his hands. He looked past Judith, as though seeing other days, other years. "At one time . . . yes, Missus Connell," he said quietly. "But no longer. I have found that there is a limit to hate, both in time and quantity . . . that no matter how a man clings to it and tries to keep it alive, it becomes a shriveled and empty husk. Under different circumstances this might not be true. It is in this case."

Judith waited, almost breathlessly, for him to go on.

"When the word first reached me," said John

Ogden, "that a member of the gang responsible for the death of my son at the Round Mountain affair had been picked up, I knew an unholy satisfaction. I couldn't cover country fast enough in my eagerness to face that man, to exact vengeance. I expected to face a typical renegade. Instead, I met your husband, a man liked and respected by those who knew him, a hard-working man of family and possessions, a man who looked me in the eye and admitted freely his part in the affair with a straightforward story of what had happened and how. Despite my desire to believe otherwise, I had to admit that there was no viciousness in Jerry Connell, that his part in the affair had been a very minor one and due entirely to the heedless recklessness of youth."

Judith drew a deep breath. "That . . . that is true, Mister Ogden. Jerry had no hand in the death of your son. He did no shooting. . . ."

"I know." John Ogden's glance came back to her and a grave smile softened the harsh lines of his face. "I heard of Jerry Connell's family and I wanted to meet them. It is a very fine one. And I felt, after being the cause of so much anxiety and worry to you, Missus Connell, that I should be the one to bring you direct word that I am withdrawing all my charges against your husband, that I will not attempt to prosecute him in any way. I might add that I have enough influence to bring this about. As soon as I return to town, I am advising Judge Masterson to free your husband and send him home to you and the children. His future and his name are clear, Missus Connell."

For a moment Judith could not think of a thing to say. Tears misted her eyes and with the sudden, warm impulsiveness that was a part of her, she stepped up to John Ogden and caught one of his hands in both of hers.

"Oh . . . thank you," she choked. "You don't . . . you can't know . . . what this means. . . ."

"I think I do, Missus Connell. It also means that I'm a better man than I suspected, and happier now than I've been in a long, long time. I've regained something that I had lost. Do you mind if I have a look at what's in that cradle yonder, and then, perhaps, sit down and become acquainted with these two little chaps?" He looked down at the twins and smiled.

John Ogden thought that the look Judith gave him through her tears was one of the loveliest things he had ever seen.

"Do I mind?" she cried softly. "Do I mind . . . ?"

Still holding his hand, she led him over to the cradle.

In town, the stage from the south came jolting and creaking in, pausing just long enough in front of By Tellifer's store to toss down a thin mail-bag, before going on up to the hotel. Sheriff Cole

Ashabaugh, having just stepped out of Mize Callan's Empire House bar, spun a well-chewed cigar butt into the dust of the street, and then went along to the store, arriving there just as By Tellifer slid the meager contents of the mailbag out onto his counter top. "Anything of interest, By?" asked Ashabaugh.

Tellifer ran through the mail quickly, his moving lips spelling out the addresses. He held out an envelope. "Somethin' for Judge Masterson. You can take it up to him if you're goin' that way."

Ashabaugh glanced at the postmark. It read: *Round Mountain, New Mexico.*

Judge Masterson was in his office, pouring over a legal tome. "From Round Mountain, Judge," said Ashabaugh as he handed the letter across the desk. "But not a word from Dave Wall, though."

Using precision and an oversize pair of scissors, Judge Masterson snipped a thin sliver of paper off the end of the envelope, pulled out the enclosure, and glanced swiftly through it. He laid it slowly down on the desk.

"A demand for the immediate extradition of Jerry Connell, Sheriff . . . backed by the requisite authority. We've used up all the time we could. I guess this is it." The judge sounded sober and a little tired.

Cole Ashabaugh took a couple of turns up and down the office, then paused at the window, looking out. "Been afraid of it all along," he said gruffly. "It was expecting too much that we'd locate this Big George Yearly in time to do any good. So I guess my fine theory wasn't so good, after all. I know that Dave Wall has done his best, but he hasn't even come up with Luke Lilavelt yet. If he had, we'd have known about it by this time. So Jerry will have to go, and that's going to be rough all around . . . damned rough."

"I'll see that he has good legal counsel," said the judge. "We'll fight John Ogden to the last breath, and on his own ground."

Outside, the sun had gone down. The dust of the street seemed to have turned gray. For that matter, thought Cole Ashabaugh savagely, the whole world had turned gray and dismal. He started to turn away from the window, stopped, stared. A low exclamation broke from him.

Judge Masterson was reading over the recently arrived item of correspondence again. His head jerked up. "What is it, Sheriff?"

"Out there . . . coming up the street. It's Dave Wall, and he's got a man with him. But it's not Luke Lilavelt."

Cole Ashabaugh left at a run and reached his own office just as Dave Wall reined to a halt in front of it. Wall's face was dark with sun and unshaven whiskers, craggy and gaunt from fatigue. His eyes were deeply sunken, gritty from loss of sleep.

The man he had with him was tied to the saddle, wrists to the horn, ankles to the cinch rings. A big man who had once been round with fat, but who seemed to have shriveled in some strange way so that flesh lay in folds and sags on him. Particularly were his jowls pouched and baggy and a livid bruise still banded his throat. In fleshy pits the man's eyes glittered with a sullen ferocity, a trapped wildness.

Almost stupidly, Ashabaugh blurted: "Who in hell is that, Dave?"

Wall stepped from his saddle as though the stiffness of a thousand years rode him. "That," he said quietly, "is Big George Yearly. Your hunch was right, Cole."

Words broke from the prisoner with a guttural thickness, as though his vocal cords were rusty from long disuse. "He's crazy . . . crazy as hell. My name is Dell . . . Hippo Dell. I demand . . . !"

"Don't demand too much, Yearly," cut in Dave Wall. "You'll get plenty as it is. Let's get him inside and out of sight, Cole. Coming in across the desert I did some thinking of my own. Maybe we can make a trade, a trade with Mister John Ogden, if we don't show our hole card too soon."

They untied the big man, hustled him inside. Cole Ashabaugh got a lamp going and its glow fought back the thickening twilight gloom in the room. With the lamp burning to his satisfaction,

Ashabaugh turned to Dave Wall. "What about Luke Lilavelt? You find him?"

Wall was silent for a moment, then shrugged. "I found him. He's dead. If you could get Judge Masterson down here, I'll give you the whole story."

"That," said Ashabaugh, "I can do, too." He went out, hurrying.

Wall pushed a chair toward his prisoner, settled back in another one himself, blinking owlishly at the lamp. He wondered at his lack of feeling. He should, he realized, feel all the uplift of a great exultation over this, for it meant the answers to so many things. But he didn't feel any uplift at all. He felt nothing more than the wish that he could crawl off in some quiet corner somewhere and sleep for a month. So much could a grinding fatigue blunt a man's sensibility. Mechanically he got out tobacco and papers and built a smoke. That didn't bring any satisfaction, either. All his senses seemed to have dried up in him, including the one of taste. He could feel the prisoner watching him, with a black and steady hatred.

In his office up street, Judge Masterson stared at Cole Ashabaugh. "You mean to say, Sheriff, that Dave Wall has actually brought in Big George Yearly?"

"So he claims," said Ashabaugh. "He wants you to hear the story, Judge."

"And I want to hear it. This is more than fortuitous. It borders on the incredible."

As they hurried along the street, a buckboard came rolling, with John Ogden driving. It went along to the livery barn and pulled up there.

Judge Masterson tipped his head toward Ogden. "If Wall is correct in this, Sheriff, it means that that man's cup of vengeance is filled to over-flowing."

They turned in at Ashabaugh's office. Dave Wall, rousing from his apathy of weariness, pulled himself to his feet. Judge Masterson took a look at the prisoner and then turned to Wall. "Sheriff Ashabaugh tells me you bring startling news, Mister Wall?"

"Yes," said Wall quietly. "I hope it will straighten things out for us. We should be able to wangle a trade with John Ogden."

"I hope so," said the judge, "for just a few minutes ago I received a communication that just about forces my hand with Jerry Connell."

A step sounded at the office door. It was John Ogden. He came in, tall and grave of face. "I don't want to intrude on something that is no concern of mine, gentlemen," he said. "But I saw you turn in here, Judge Masterson, and if you'll spare me time for a word or two, it will save me bothering you later."

The judge looked at him sternly. "Very well. What is it?"

"I have just returned from the Connell Ranch. I thought you might like to know that I have reconsidered. I am not going to push my demand for the extradition of Jerry Connell, nor will I move to prosecute him in any way. I have come to realize that bringing further unhappiness to him and his family would bring no satisfaction at all to me. I have spoken to Missus Connell, spent an hour with her and her children. They deserve much more than the empty vengeance of a tired and bitter man. I recommend that Jerry Connell be immediately released from custody and sent back to his family."

For a long moment the room was very still. After all they had feared from John Ogden, this quiet, sincere statement left Dave Wall, the judge, and Cole Ashabaugh momentarily stunned. Judge Masterson recovered first. A warm smile broke across his fine face and he stepped quickly over to Ogden, hand outstretched.

"I would like to congratulate you, sir . . . and shake your hand. I believe I can say with all truthfulness that you'll now find a happiness you have long missed."

John Ogden smiled as they struck hands. "I have already found it. Perhaps I might have felt differently if Connell was directly responsible for the death of my son. But I am thoroughly convinced now that he was not. The man truly responsible is still at large, somewhere."

Dave Wall cleared his throat. "We have a surprise for you, Mister Ogden. We are prepared to deliver that man to you."

John Ogden reared his head and shoulders to that tall erectness, and his eyes grew piercing. "You mean . . . you know the whereabouts of Big George Yearly?"

Wall pointed. "There he sits."

Ogden turned and looked at Hippo Dell. The muscles of Ogden's lean jaws crawled into little knots of tension. Under the impact of Ogden's hard stare, Hippo's sullen glowering showed a faint break. He blurted words he'd already uttered: "He's crazy. My name is Dell!"

Ogden turned to Wall again. "You have proof?"

"I think so. See what you think." Wall pinched out the butt of his cigarette and began speaking, moving slowly and with care, to keep everything in sequence. He sketched Cole Ashabaugh's theory as to how Luke Lilavelt had managed to get hold of the Wanted dodger on Jerry Connell, and how Lilavelt had used the dodger as a club over him. "We hoped that by locating Lilavelt and making him talk, we could pick up the trail of Big George Yearly," he explained. "So I set out to run down Lilavelt."

He told of the trails he had ridden in this effort and where they had led him. He told of how through Wind River, the old cook at the Pinnacle spread, he had finally got a fairly direct line on how to locate Lilavelt.

"Wind River gave me the right steer, all right. The man everybody knew as Hippo Dell did show up in Crater City, hoping to get word from Hub Magley that one of Lilavelt's gunfighters had done my business for me. I trailed Dell into the desert and he led me to Lilavelt."

Wall told of crawling up through the night to the rim of the desert wash above Lilavelt's camp. He told of the words that passed between Lilavelt and Hippo Dell.

"I couldn't believe my ears at first when I heard Lilavelt call this fellow I'd known as Dell by another name, by the tag that made him George Yearly. They quarreled over that. Yearly was savage about it. He warned Lilavelt never to name him so again. He said that the name George Yearly was done with, forgotten . . . and that only Hippo Dell remained." Wall paused, rubbed a hand across his bristly jaw. "Well, I heard enough. It all tied in . . . it all made sense . . . it supplied all the missing parts. So then it was up to me to get Yearly back here . . . to Basin. And alive. So I waited it out, until they'd gone to sleep. Then I tried to sneak in. Lilavelt woke up, yelled an alarm, started shooting. I shot back. I killed Lilavelt. Then I tackled Yearly before he could get clear of his blankets. I managed to get the best of him and . . . there he is."

While Wall had been speaking, some of the stolidity had gone out of Hippo Dell. He stirred restlessly on his chair and Cole Ashabaugh, drifting a little nearer the door, watched him intently. John Ogden and Judge Masterson were also staring at Hippo.

"Damnedest mess of lies I ever listened to," blurted Hippo. "I tell you, my name is Hippo Dell. Just because Wall claims different doesn't make it so."

"You've a point there," said Judge Masterson quietly. "Er . . . you admit, however, that you and Lilavelt did have this camp in the desert?"

"Sure we did. That was Lilavelt's idea. He was afraid of Wall, for Wall had made his brag that he intended to kill Lilavelt. Me, I just worked for Lilavelt. If he wanted to hide out in the desert, that was his business."

"But Lilavelt was hoping to get word from this Hub Magley to the effect that some Window Sash hand had managed to kill Wall?" probed the Judge.

"Sure he was. Knowing that Wall was out to get him, you couldn't blame Lilavelt for trying to see that somebody got Wall first. Far as I was concerned, it was all right with me to play messenger boy. I was drawing wages from Lilavelt, and if I hadn't been on that job, I'd have been working on another for him somewhere else."

"What is your version of what took place out at that desert camp?"

"I'd been into Crater City for some grub and to see if there was any word from Hub Magley," said Hippo. "When I got back to camp, Lilavelt was some worried because there'd been no word from Magley. I went ahead and cooked supper. Then me and Lilavelt sat around and smoked for a while. We turned in a little later. Next thing I knew a shot woke me up. Right after that this Wall *hombre* landed on me and tried to choke me to death. He didn't . . . quite. But he tied me up and brought me in here, telling me I was a guy named Big George Yearly. Hell, I don't even know what it's all about. Except that Wall's cooked up some crazy scheme to cover up the fact that he killed Luke Lilavelt while he lay asleep. Shot him to death in his blankets without giving Lilavelt a chance."

John Ogden, a silent and expressionless listener, turned to Dave Wall. "I'm forming no opinions, jumping at no conclusions. But after coming this far and in light of the change that has taken place within me, I want to be very sure in this matter. I'm questioning no one's word. But it does seem some further burden of proof exists in this matter, Mister Wall."

"I think that can be supplied," Wall assured. "Jerry Connell hasn't laid eyes on Big George Yearly since the night of that affair at Round

Mountain, years ago. He has no idea that I just rode in with that man. Cole, go bring Jerry in. Don't say a word to him. Nobody will say a word to him. Just bring him in and let him look around. Go ahead, Cole . . . I'll keep an eye on our friend yonder."

Cole Ashabaugh nodded and went along the hall that led from the rear of the office to the jail. Dave Wall built another cigarette. Judge Masterson and John Ogden moved over against the side of the room, stood quietly.

Jerry came in, blinking against the lamplight. He'd lost weight and his face was drawn. He saw Dave Wall and exclaimed: "Dave! Where you been? What . . . ?"

Jerry broke off abruptly. His anxious glance, moving past Wall, had touched the big, gross figure of Hippo Dell and Hippo seemed to crouch, like a burly animal ready to spring. Jerry's glance, full upon Hippo now, held and held. His lips moved, but no sound came forth at first. But finally words did come, slowly and spaced, as though from the lips of a man completely dazed. "Big George Yearly. Big . . . George . . . Yearly. . . ."

"I guess," said John Ogden harshly, "I guess that's it."

Chapter Twelve

Half an hour later, Dave Wall, Judge Masterson, and Cole Ashabaugh were alone in the sheriff's office. Jerry Connell, hardly able to believe the benevolent turn that fortune had taken, was on his way home. John Ogden had gone over to the hotel. Big George Yearly was securely locked in the same cell that had held Jerry Connell.

Judge Masterson, searching his pockets fruitlessly for a pipe that he'd left on his own desk, accepted a cheroot from Cole Ashabaugh and lit up. Dave Wall spoke wearily.

"One last angle to be cleared up." He looked at the sheriff. "I promised you, Cole, that I'd bring Luke Lilavelt in alive. Instead, I killed him. Where does that leave me?"

Ashabaugh cleared his throat, stepped to the open door, and spat out into the darkness. "Didn't have any choice, did you?" he answered gruffly. "Lilavelt threw the first shot, didn't he? Well then, do you think I'd expect you to be fool enough to stand there and let him keep shooting until he made one good? Judge, what do you think?"

"Clearly a case of self-defense," said the judge crisply. "Besides, Lilavelt had put out orders to his riders that they were to get you at

248

first chance, hadn't he? I see no cause for the slightest concern on your part, Mister Wall."

"Thanks," said Wall bleakly. "But I'll probably know concern for a long time. For it marks the dark end of a dark trail. I've a lot of forgetting to do."

The judge dropped a hand on Wall's arm. "It's been a trail few men would have been big enough and generous enough to travel. Remember, given time, all things pass. And even the darkest shadows are formed by the sunlight that lies beyond." The judge brought out a heavy gold case watch, snapped open the cover, and glanced at it. And for the first time Cole Ashabaugh could remember, he heard Judge Masterson swear.

"Damn! It's 'way past my suppertime."

The judge hurried out. Cole Ashabaugh pointed to the bunk in a far corner. "Get over on that and forget everything," he ordered. "I'll take care of your horses. When was the last time you had a real night's sleep?"

Dave Wall stretched and yawned, moved stiffly over to the bunk. "I've forgotten." He pulled off his boots and flattened out. Sleep hit him like a club.

Morning's sunlight filtered the room when he awoke. Cigarette smoke was in the air. Dave Wall turned his head and saw Tres Debley sitting in Cole Ashabaugh's desk chair, his feet cocked high. Tres said: "Time you woke up. I been hearing the damnedest things. Are they all true?"

Wall grinned. "Depends. Man, I'm hungry."

Tres said: "Same here. There's a place up the street that looks pretty good. Come on."

Over their belated breakfast they swapped stories. Tres's was brief enough. He'd found nothing out at the Crimson Hills headquarters and after returning to Crater City had got the message Wall had left with Charlie Ring. "So then," ended Tres, "I headed for Basin. And missed all the fun," he added disgustedly.

"No fun," said Wall bluntly, then told Tres all about it. "You can forget Hippo Dell . . . or, better, George Yearly. He's got a ride ahead of him I wouldn't want to face. Now me for a bath and a shave and a new outfit of clothes. Got to mark a fresh start all around."

Tres spun a cigarette, inhaled deeply. "Nearly forgot. Got a message for you. Had a visit with some friends of yours back in the Crimson Hills country. The Suttons. I was told to tell you not to forget them. It was a pretty emphatic order."

"Yeah," murmured Wall. "Who gave it?"

"Tracy did," said Tres with studied casualness.

Wall thought about that while he dickered with By Tellifer for the new outfit of clothes. He thought about it while he lay back in Sam Lange's barber chair while Sam's shears and razor worked busily. He thought about it while he soaked and steamed for an hour in Sam's bathroom out back. Later, feeling a new man inside and out, he went in search of Tres and found him swapping idle talk with Cole Ashabaugh in the latter's office. Cole shaded his eyes with his hand.

"Can't be the same feller, Debley. This one shines."

"You go to hell." Wall grinned. "Tres, you can drift out to the ranch and kill time there for a week or two. You'll hear from me. Tell Judith and Jerry I'll be along to see them before too long."

"You," said Tres, as though he didn't know, "sound like you were going somewhere."

"And you can join Cole on the same journey," retorted Wall. "Be seeing you."

He went away, heading for the livery barn, a tall quick-striding figure, keen with the vital essence of life.

Cole Ashabaugh spoke softly. "I like that man. But I can't figure his hurry."

"I can," said Tres laconically. "He's luckier than you or I will ever be. But he's earned that luck. I'll buy a drink, Ashabaugh. It's about that time of day."

He came up out of the desert with the same driving eagerness that had carried him into it. His glance ran steadily ahead of him as he climbed the long slope that led to the bench land where

Bart Sutton's headquarters at Sweet Winds stood. The ranch house shone white while the trees that surrounded it loomed green and cool, rustling lazily in the breeze that gave the ranch its name.

He remembered the other times he'd ridden up to this same headquarters and of the action and reaction that had met him there. An awful lot had happened since that first visit. The stars of some men had risen, while those of others had fallen. Fate, luck, and some sound reasoning had tossed a great many things into the pot, but out of it all had come at last a sane, bright balance to life.

He saw her while still far off. A slim and motionless figure on the ranch house porch, and when he drew closer, she dropped lightly down the steps and came to meet him. He thought back to the first time he had seen her, on that distant day when she had ridden past him, his not knowing who she was and she entirely unaware of him. The way the wonder of her had stayed with him.

She wasn't any different now. She was the same in his eyes as she had been that day, and as she would always be. She was crisp and cool and immaculate, and her eyes were shining. She spoke simply.

"Dave. I knew that if I waited and watched the desert trail long enough, then one day you would come riding."

He swung down and she stood close to him, her hands in his. "A greeting like this . . . for me . . . for Dave Wall?" he said.

A little tremor was in her soft, glad laughter and a swift mist touched her eyes. "I know all about Dave Wall. Tres Debley told Dad and me all about you . . . why you rode for Luke Lilavelt . . . everything. But that wouldn't have mattered anyhow. Nothing would have."

They walked over to the ranch house, hand in hand. Bart Sutton, looking much his old self, stood in the doorway and his deep voice rang gladly.

"Boy . . . you've come home!"

About the Author

L.P. Holmes was the author of a number of outstanding Western novels. Born in a snowed-in log cabin in the heart of the Rockies near Breckenridge, Colorado, Holmes moved with his family when very young to northern California and it was there that his father and older brothers built the ranch house where Holmes grew up and where, in later life, he would live again. He published his first story—"The Passing of the Ghost"—in *Action Stories* (9/25). He was paid ½¢ a word and received a check for $40. "Yeah . . . forty bucks," he said later. "Don't laugh. In those far-off days . . . a pair of young parents with a three-year-old son could buy a lot of groceries on forty bucks." He went on to contribute nearly six hundred stories of varying lengths to the magazine market as well as to write numerous Western novels. For many years of his life, Holmes would write in the mornings and spend his afternoons calling on a group of friends in town, among them the blind Western author, Charles H. Snow, who Lew Holmes always called Judge Snow (because he was Napa's Justice of the Peace in 1920–1924) and who frequently makes an appearance in later novels as a local justice in Holmes's imaginary Western communities. Holmes produced such notable novels as *Somewhere They Die* (1955) for which he received the Spur Award from the Western Writers of America. *The Sunset Trail* (2014), a California riverboat story, marked his most recent appearance. In L.P. Holmes's stories one finds the themes so basic to his Western fiction: the loyalty that unites one man to another, the pride one must take in his work and a job well done, the innate generosity of most of the people who live in Holmes's ambient Western communities, and the vital relationship between a man and a woman in making a better life.

Center Point Large Print
600 Brooks Road / PO Box 1
Thorndike, ME 04986-0001 USA

(207) 568-3717

US & Canada:
1 800 929-9108
www.centerpointlargeprint.com